Pursuit of Bliss

Other books by Betty Palmer Nelson

From the series Honest Women

Private Knowledge
The Weight of Light

Pursuit of Bliss

1913 to 1919

Betty Palmer Nelson

St. Martin's Press/New York

Library of Congress Cataloging-in-Publication Data

Nelson, Betty Palmer.
    Pursuit of bliss / Betty Palmer Nelson.
       p.   cm.
    ISBN 0-312-08169-3 (hardcover)
    ISBN 0-312-11049-9 (paperback)
    I. Title.
  PS3564.E429P8   1992   92-25156
  813'.54—dc20   CIP

First Paperback Edition: April 1994

10 9 8 7 6 5 4 3 2 1

For my mother and father, Bertha Catherine Proctor Palmer and George Duncan Palmer, with gratitude and love always

Arcite says when released from prison:

Alas, why do we commonly complain
About what God provides, or fickle Fortune,
That often gives to us in many a guise
Much better than we can ourselves devise?
One man desires the most to have great richness
That causes his own murder or great sickness;
Another thinks escape from prison gain
Who, free at home, is by his family slain.
Infinite harms we will in such a matter.
We know not what we pray—we merely chatter;
We fare like one who's drunk as any mouse:
A drunken man knows well he has a house,
But how to get there straight he cannot see,
For to a drunk all paths are slippery.
Now in our lives we all behave like this;
We run all day pursuing hard our bliss,
But we go wrong full often, certainly.

—Chaucer, ''The Knight's Tale,'' *The Canterbury Tales*

Ingmar Bergman's *Seventh Seal*

Silence must be the answer
To those who ask for God,
Except for occasional strawberries
And breath and bone and blood.

Contents

Principal Families

This is the third novel in the Honest Women series. The Hendersons and Armstrongs-Gwaltneys appear in the first two, *Private Knowledge* and *The Weight of Light*. This genealogy presents them as they first appear in *Pursuit of Bliss* and omits some characters in these families from the earlier novels.

Cutterfields

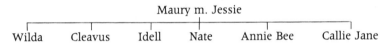

Maury m. Jessie

| Wilda | Cleavus | Idell | Nate | Annie Bee | Callie Jane |

Hendersons

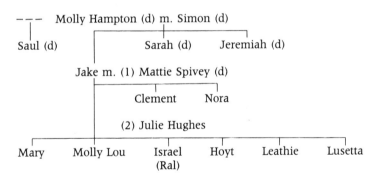

– – – Molly Hampton (d) m. Simon (d)

Saul (d)

Sarah (d)   Jeremiah (d)

Jake m. (1) Mattie Spivey (d)

Clement   Nora

(2) Julie Hughes

| Mary | Molly Lou | Israel (Ral) | Hoyt | Leathie | Lusetta |

Gwaltneys

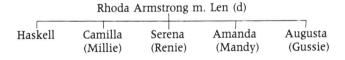

Rhoda Armstrong m. Len (d)

| Haskell | Camilla (Millie) | Serena (Renie) | Amanda (Mandy) | Augusta (Gussie) |

Pursuit of Bliss

Prologue: Thunder

Granny is afraid of thunderstorms. She always associ-
ates them with the tornado, or cyclone as she called it, which
she lived through in Tarpley when she was five years old. It
came on a March night when the daffodils' trumpets and
spring thunderstorms arrive together in Tennessee to an-
nounce the disruption of winter's quiet. There are no deep
snows lying in the woods here to tempt the traveler to stop his
journey. But there is a brown evenness to winter life, from the
low grass to the twigs of the highest trees. When the daffodils
and thunderstorms come, the twigs turn red and yellow with
the life racing under their bark. This is the time of year that
horses founder from too much green, silky, new grass after a
long winter of nothing but dry hay.

Granny's mother, Jessie, had called the children all in from
playing hide-and-seek in the dusk after supper and had
shooed them—their father, too—into the cellar, as she al-

ways did when a storm was coming. They had cowered there among the bushels of turnips and potatoes, listening to the thunderclaps and downpour draw nearer, then pass.

Just as they were about to leave their shelter, her mother said, "Wait! There's more coming!" And they could hear it, getting louder and louder.

Her father said, "Sounds for the world like a thrashing machine, but it can't be this time of year."

Then it was so loud no one could hear what anybody said, and they were all listening too hard to talk anyhow.

When the noise had passed, they heard rain again, and after waiting a few minutes and wondering if it was safe to come out, they opened the cellar door. Granny's eight-year-old brother Nate, always impatient of confinement, rushed out. He yelled, "It's all right! It's just raining!" Then they all dashed through the rain-cold dark to the kitchen door and went to bed.

The next morning, Pap called them for milking and opened the door to go out and start himself. Then he shouted, "Lord have mercy! Jessie! Children! Come here! The barn's gone!"

There were the mower and plows in their places and the cows standing looking at the hoof-dented earth where their stalls and hay had been. There were a few stall walls and mangers left, and some of the hay from the loft lay in heaps here and there over the yard and garden. A clump of uprooted daffodils—buttercups, Granny always called them—lay in one of the mangers. But the logs, boards, and shingles, and even the beams and rafters that had made the barn, were gone, as though a broom had swept them away in the night.

Then the five-year-old child that became Granny had looked up as if expecting to see the barn lifted whole into the air. Instead, in the elm tree she saw something else. At first she could do nothing but point, but then she screamed, and they all looked first at her, then at the woman hanging in the tree, caught in the limbs twenty feet up, naked even to her bloomers, her long, bare breasts and loose hair hanging down in the gray light before sunrise. It was the first dead person Granny had ever seen. Her mother snatched her up and carried her inside, but she still saw the woman whenever she closed her eyes.

The tornado had swept through the east side of the county, but it had hit only two buildings: the Cutterfields' barn and the Lovells' house. Mrs. Lovell's family came to claim her body as soon as they got word; Pap and a neighbor had taken it down from the tree. Neighbors brought back some of the tack that had been blown away. They also brought back some things that didn't belong to the Cutterfields, blown from who knew where. They helped build back the barn, too. And the Lovells' house.

After that, whenever there was a thunderstorm, Granny was the first one to notice. She smelled rain in the air sooner than her father could. And even in the dead of night, she was the first one awake when a storm broke. But before she would go to the cellar, she dressed completely, even down to shoes and socks. And when she was grown, she always awoke her own children, my mother Clara and her brother, and made them do the same.

Long after her children in turn were grown and gone, one July afternoon Granny went down to the cellar by herself to weather a thunderstorm. She had her other routines established, of course; she always left a chair under the cobweb-draped overhead light and had brought her cup of coffee and newly delivered newspaper. By then she usually read the obituaries first, then turned to what she called the foreign news, which meant anything farther away than Nashville. She didn't notice the storm outside so much if she could turn to other kinds of storms.

Before she had read very far, she glanced up toward the cans of tomatoes, blackberries, beans, pickles, and preserves gleaming like jewels on the cellar shelves, and she saw a snake there. It didn't take her long to debate between her fears of the snake and the storm; she was out in the rain and inside the house without seeing it move. She sent my grandfather down to the cellar when he came in, to turn out the light and bring up her paper, she told him; they both knew it was to find the snake and kill it. He didn't that day, but she sent him down to bring up the cans of food often enough afterward that he did kill it soon and brought it up to show her. Then she'd go back down again herself, but not without sweeping the whole cellar with her flashlight as she came down the steps.

When I was a child visiting her, gathering the eggs was always a high point of the day. There seemed more magic in finding a smooth, perfect ovoid in its straw nest than in gathering, say, tomatoes that had been planted, watered, hoed, and watched through slow days as they swelled from blossoms and turned red; the eggs seemed like gifts, unexpected treasures. But Granny always warned me to poke a stick into the nests that were above my slight height: there could be a snake waiting there for an unwary hand. Even shed skins were to be shunned.

Her own sheddings, the hair she loosed when she combed out her long braids, were carefully collected in a cloth spread out over her knees. When she had done her hair up again, she always made a small bundle of the loose hairs and poked them through the latticework around the crawl space under the porch. I knew from the time that I was very young that she did that to keep from getting a headache, the sure consequence of letting a bird find her hair and incorporate it in its nest.

One of the debts I owe my mother is her not passing on the unreasoning fears my grandmother gave her. I knew when I was a girl that whenever there was a thunderstorm at night, Mother always got up and sat by herself in the dark, but she never woke us. She never voluntarily touched a worm, much less a snake, but she didn't stop my father from handing me a grass snake to feel the cool, dry scales.

She wasn't able to hide her fears. When I was in elementary school, I saw her slap a neighbor child before she could stop herself for dropping a tobacco worm, translucent green and fat, onto her arm. When I was a little older, I saw her reach into a barrel to get cracked corn to feed the chickens, and when a mouse ran up her coatsleeve, she screamed and shook it out. Reaching back into the barrel, she felt another,

4

and the coat came off regardless of the December cold as she ran out of the hen house.

So I know her fears but do not share them. I have fears of my own. I have refused to cross an I-beam footbridge even to see the path of a Swiss glacier because the bridge had no side rails. When my family and I were driving along the crest of a hogback ridge in Utah and stopped to see the view, I refused to leave the car but sat as though holding it down by my weight on the narrow shoulder of the highway three thousand feet above the valleys on both sides. Surely this acrophobia is as unreasoning as staying awake to fend off the harmless sound of thunder or the unavoidable but unlikely harm of lightning or tornado.

And then there is my greatest fear, the fear that I shall miss my life, realize some day that I have through the little everyday fears of disruption, conflict, rejection, embarrassment, and poverty avoided views more spectacular than Switzerland and Utah, vistas of my own soul or those of others or of what we call God.

As a young teenager, I was afflicted even more than most (I think now with middle-aged self-centeredness) with what we call shyness, the love of self that makes us think everyone else is as interested in us as we are but knows all our blemishes, depravity, and ignorance as well as we do, too. I had spent a good bit of my efforts during a week-long summer camp flirting with the kind of boy I usually chose as object of my affections—one older and "smooth" around the opposite sex, already "going steady" with someone else and automatically elected to the first of whatever offices were open—in other words, someone sure not to notice me, much less return my interest.

But to my surprise, Mark did. He spent his time at the crafts booth with me instead of at the archery range with Nancy, his erstwhile steady. My confidantes, girls my own age, of course, all assured me that success was mine. "Evelyn, he *likes* you. Why don't you flirt with him more?" I responded that I would, but the truth was that I was already doing all I knew how to and was brave enough to.

At the Friday-night dance, he sought me out. "Want to dance?"

"Sure." The monosyllable strained my strength.

We did reels first, then began square-dancing. The fast pace saved me from the necessity of conversation, but when the set ended, the caller said, "Now, fellows, keep that pretty girl for your own."

Mark, still holding my hand, said, "Guess that's you."

I was flooded with gratitude and regret. For I knew it all: knew that he had given me a priceless gift, that to smile and nod my head would be enough to claim it, that not to respond would be the cruelest thing I had ever done to anyone and would surely drive him away, and that nothing was exactly what I was going to do, despite him and myself. My fear paralyzed me, kept me even from looking at him.

He left. Fortunately, we all went to our separate homes the next morning, and I never saw him again.

I have wished that I could have let him know how I felt, the sweet onrush of pleasure in the world that he gave me. But my cowardice stopped me; I was afraid of thunder.

Yet even then I knew that thunder comes with the rain that sweetens the air and waters the growing plants of spring. And if it sometimes comes with lightning and wind, well, that's what courage and endurance are for.

Book One

*The Heart Asks
Pleasure First
1913 to 1914*

I. Growing Up

To wait through dinner was almost impossible for Annie Bee. Nate wasn't there, and she was glad; he had told Mammy that he was going over to Gavin O'Neill's to help breed a heifer and had shot Annie Bee a leer. If he had sat across from her for the whole long meal, she probably would have let everything out.

She had cooked the cornbread, beans, mustard greens, and side meat for dinner because Mammy had been up most of the night catching Mrs. Marva Conyer's twins, the topic of the conversation for an indecent length of time.

Mammy said, "They're just as cute as buttons, but not much bigger. She's going to name them Seth and Sewell. Have some more beans, Maury."

Pap dipped from the bowl while he talked. "Well, Seth's old Mr. Conyer's grandaddy's name on his mother's side, but where'd she get the Sewell?"

"Reckon that's the name of a man who courted her before she met Winchell. Arlene and the rest of the Conyers are right put out that she'd name one of Winchell's younguns for him. Arlene even hinted maybe they *wasn't* Winchell's. But looks to me like they've got the Conyer eyes. And their big ears. But then Arlene ain't never cared much for Marva; Winchell was her baby, and she wanted to keep him home for herself."

Pap speared a piece of meat. "Besides, twins runs in the Conyer family. They've already got Lujean and Lucinda for grandbabies, and that bunch over to Cranston's got twin boys. Annie Bee, baby, fetch me some more of that cold buttermilk, please. Seems like nothing else don't cool a man so much on a hot day."

As Annie Bee got up and turned to get the buttermilk jug off the wash stand, Callie Jane quit feeding her face long enough to join the conversation. "Annie Bee's washed her hair again. It's not been more'n a week since the last time she washed it."

Annie Bee wished for the millionth time that Callie Jane had never been born, or at least that she hadn't survived to reach the age of thirteen, at which age she felt grown-up enough to say whatever she thought, whether it was any of her business or not. "I've had some dandruff lately, and I thought while I took Wednesday bath, I'd just wash it too." At least she had her answer ready. She had thought about braiding her hair up again so no one would notice but knew it would never dry that way, not in Tennessee, where Pap said a body could wring the water out of the air if he could just grab hold.

Mammy said, "You really ought not wash your hair too often, Annie Bee; the soap dries all the oil out of the scalp and takes the shine."

"I didn't use lye soap, Mammy; I bought some Castile soap last time I was at the store. And I rinsed it with vinegar too."

"Well, I wondered what you'd done with the money you got from picking blackberries. I hope you don't fritter it all away on fancy things we could do without; lye soap's good enough for washing bodies and hair too."

"She probably used up all the rainwater too, and Saturday's the day I'm supposed to wash my hair. If it don't rain between now and Saturday, I'll have to use old hard water on mine." Callie Jane looked aggrieved.

"I did not. There's plenty of rainwater left in the barrel for yours. Though that's not going to help your old red kinky stuff anyhow."

Pap tried to make peace. "Now, girls, you both have pretty hair. Annie Bee, yours is just like your mammy's. Jessie, you've still got the prettiest head of hair I ever seen."

Callie Jane started crying and left the table. Annie Bee felt smug about both Callie Jane's departure and the compliment to herself, although she had never thought about Mammy's hair being pretty; it was black and thick like her own, but streaked with white above her ears.

Mammy sighed and looked after Callie Jane but turned back to the business at hand. "What are you going to do with the rest of your blackberry money, child?"

Annie Bee had the answer for that ready too, had thought of it long ago. "Mrs. Henderson's making me a dress. A white-and-blue one, for good." Every word was true; she didn't have to say how good.

"Well, it sure is kind of Mrs. Henderson to sew for you as well as Leathie. After Wilda and Idell got big enough, I depended on them to sew for us all, I was gone so much with the midwifing. Now that they're married and gone, I've practically forgot how to sew decent. But Mrs. Henderson does a beautiful job."

"I may go see Leathie a while this afternoon." That too was true as far as it went.

"Well, that's all right, I reckon; Ral's probably working in the fields today. But I'd just as soon you didn't go running over there all the time long as Israel Henderson's courting you. Folks'll talk."

Not much longer they won't, Annie Bee thought. *Not after a week or so. And after today, it won't matter.*

Fighting the July heat in the tiny bedroom that she shared with Callie Jane, she stripped to her bloomers and shimmy while she braided her hair. She wound the two plaits around her head and covered them in the front with her unbraided forelock, tucking the long length underneath the braids. Then she tied a white cloth around her head to keep any hair from straying.

She was satisfied. Pap had gone back to his cornfield, and Mammy had gone to sleep in her rocker on the front porch the way she did every day after dinner if she had been out catching a baby the night before. Callie Jane had prissed off to the store. All this summer, afraid she was an old maid at thirteen, almost every afternoon she had gone to flirt with anybody in pants that happened to be there. And the dress pleased Annie Bee, too; it looked just the way that she had imagined when she told Mrs. Henderson what she wanted—insertion with blue ribbons breaking up the white batiste at the neckline, the deep square yoke, the waist, and the sleeves. Ral liked for her to wear blue to match her eyes, which were deep blue like all the Cutterfields'.

Something blue, something new. She had plenty old, that was sure; she had made only enough money picking blackberries to buy the material and trims for the dress, not the new kid shoes she wanted at Nolan's or new underwear or gowns. Well, the underclothes and gowns wouldn't matter much; Ral certainly hadn't seen any of hers yet anyhow.

She imagined Ral seeing her. He had always said that he liked her a little chuffy, and she knew by that he meant the fullness of her breasts. He would like her hips, too, she thought, then looked away from that part of her body.

Her freckles certainly showed up, not so many as Callie Jane had, of course, but everyone expects freckles with red hair. Why should she have to have them too? But though she always wore a bonnet to keep the sun off, they were there, not red like Callie Jane's, but definitely there, rose-beige specks all down her arms and shoulders. She knew they also floated under the pale skin of her nose and cheeks like fallen leaves sinking under the creek water. But she would cover those with face powder. She hoped that it wouldn't cake in this weather.

Something borrowed. That was the lace handkerchief Leathie had lent her, the one Nate had bought when he had gone to Nashville with Ral, Hoyt, and Joe Conyer. Leathie was almost as excited as Annie Bee. She kept saying that after the wedding, they would be real sisters, and then when she married Nate, they would be more than sisters—double sisters.

Annie Bee had warned her that if she wanted to marry Nate, she would have to be firm with him. That's what she had done with Ral—told him he would have to marry her if he wanted to keep her. If he wasn't old enough at twenty-four to settle down, he never would be. And sixteen was old enough for her, too, no matter what Mammy and Pap thought.

Mostly Mammy. Pap had never told her "No," never even said "Wait," any time she had ever asked for anything. Although she hadn't quite asked him if she could marry Ral— indeed, she had told Ral that he *couldn't* ask her parents—she was sure Pap wouldn't keep anything she truly wanted away from her. But Mammy was different.

Annie Bee frowned as she carefully pulled the black silk stockings up almost to her knees and rolled them around her garters. They had cost a dear price and would run at the least little snag, but she would have paid her last cent to get them.

Nate and Leathie. They would be at the O'Neills' when she got there. Nate was the only one of her family that she had told. He was the one that she would miss the most, too, when she quit living at home. He was three years older, and she couldn't remember a day in her life that they had not been together. As children they had fought and hated and protected and loved each other; Nate had never gotten a whipping that she hadn't cried about, even when she had tattled to get him punished in the first place. They had spent days on end in the woods, swinging from grapevines into the creek, snaring and roasting small animals, looking for nuts and berries, climbing trees that they pretended were the masts of tall ships like in the picture of Old Ironsides in the schoolhouse. She had gone to school more than he, for he had to work in the fields during summer when school was kept. So she taught him her lessons at night; it hadn't seemed right for her to know more than he did. Now her decision to marry would lead her away from him. She saw him alone in the woods of their childhood.

The dress fit her perfectly. But of course Mrs. Henderson had made clothes for her for years—ever since she and Leathie had thought of dressing alike. And Ral had paid no attention to his mother's making it, so it would be as if he had never seen it before. She frowned again. That was the trouble: Ral never paid much attention to anything—just went along from day to day, never planning or wanting change. Left up to him, there would be no marriage; he would never do anything but court her the way he had for the past three years till they were both old and gray.

Of course, the Hendersons weren't much of a marrying family. There were Clem and Nora, his half brother and half sister, living away back from the main road and the creek, a couple of old maids keeping house like an old married couple. And Molly Lou, who married some man named Elliott from Ridgefield and walked back home alone after two weeks. Mary was the only one really married. Ral and the other young ones were just fooling around. Even Leathie didn't seem too eager to go ahead and marry Nate. Annie Bee set her mouth. Ral at least would be settling down now.

She hated to cover the new dress with her old green one, especially in this sultry weather. But she would have to in case Mammy had finished napping and saw her. She propped her note up on the bureau. Carrying the bolster case she had packed days before and hidden under her bed, she hurried out the back door. It wouldn't do to be late.

Except for Ral and the squire, everyone was already in the O'Neills' front room when Gavin O'Neill met her at the door. "Well, well, A. B. C., with freckles clear to *Z*," he said.

She frowned at him. He had always seemed like family, for his sister Sally had married her brother Cleavus years ago. But that didn't give him the right to treat her like a little sister now. "Do you have to use that baby rhyme today?" she demanded.

"Now, Annie, don't get riled. You know I haven't said that in a long time, but it came to mind that I won't be able to after today. I can't think of anything to rhyme with 'A. B. H.' Maybe 'always has an itch'?" He laughed, and she did too. It was hard to stay angry with Gavin. Though he was a little older than Ral, he looked like a boy with his clear, cool green eyes and his halo of dark brown curls.

His wife Mary, Ral's oldest sister, rescued her and took her to the other room, the bedroom, to get ready. "Leave your night things in here, child. We'll sleep out on the porch tonight so you and Ral can have the bed."

"Oh no ma'am, we couldn't let you do that!"

"No trouble. In hot weather like this, we do sometimes anyhow."

Mary would hear of nothing else, so Annie Bee laid out her gown and toiletries. Leathie came in, and she and Mary helped Annie Bee take off the green dress and headcloth and make the minute adjustments necessary for Annie Bee's peace of mind. Mary had phlox, Queen Anne's lace, and larkspur in vases in both rooms, and she took out the lark-spur and Queen Anne's lace in the bedroom for Annie Bee to carry. "That'll go with your ribbons," she said.

"Do you know why Ral's not here yet?" Annie Bee asked.

"Oh, he is," Mary said. "We just sent him out to the barn to make sure he wouldn't see you before the wedding. But

Squire Gwaltney isn't here yet. You did give him the right time, didn't you?''

"Yes'm. I called him on the telephone last week when Mammy and Pap went to the store." Annie Bee was conscious of the distinction of having a telephone because of her mother's midwifery and of having used the strange device for her own grown-up business. She had called the squire instead of the preacher because she was afraid that the Reverend Mr. Whiston would tell Mammy and Pap.

But Mary still looked doubtful. "Are you sure he understood right? It's hard to hear on those newfangled things."

Annie Bee herself began to have misgivings, but Leathie peeked into the other room and announced that the squire had arrived, Gavin had summoned Ral from the barn, and they were all ready. Annie Bee closed her eyes and prayed silently, *Oh, Lord, make everything just the way I want it.* She checked her dress one last time and followed Mary and Leathie through the door.

As they sat at the supper Mary and Gavin had cooked, Annie Bee couldn't remember the ceremony except for Squire Gwaltney's asking, "Do you, Israel Henderson, take this woman . . . ?" Woman. She was a woman grown and married now. No one could treat her like a little girl ever again.

She loved the way Ral looked, lean and intense. He was not big like his father or his brothers Clem and Hoyt. He was not even quite as tall as Mary, though she had always been sickly and was as thin as a cornstalk. He and Leathie were small-boned like their mother, and like her they moved as secretly as a cat. Ral had his mother's heavy black hair, too. But his eyes were like his father's—the shiny, impenetrable brown of persimmon seeds stripped of their slippery caul. His mother's eyes were gray-green, full of leafy light like the spring water in the limestone pool in the Hendersons' woods.

Annie Bee wondered when she and Ral had children what color the children's eyes would be.

Squire Gwaltney, a big, solemn man who owned the best land around, had left for home right after the ceremony without staying for supper. Gavin, Leathie, and Nate joked and laughed as they ate, but they didn't tease her.

She insisted on helping to wash the dishes, and when the women finished, Leathie and Mary bedded the bride and brought Ral to her. Then they closed the bedroom door. The new couple listened as the guests left, and Mary called, "We're going out on the front porch now." The outside door banged to like a thunderclap.

Annie Bee and Ral did not talk. Ral turned out the kerosene lamp, and she listened to the sounds of his undressing and felt the springs of the bed give as he climbed in with her. Then he worked quickly, and she felt too that this was something urgent, something they had to get through because it was expected of them, something a little strange too, almost, well, even silly. Yesterday it would have been wrong. Tonight it was her duty.

His moans made her wonder if he hurt; it was kind of uncomfortable for her. But finally he came and settled down beside her with a contented sound. She thought, *This is what being married is like. Now I'm a wife.*

The next night was more satisfactory. After Ral had gone to sleep, she lay in his bed at his home—their bed in her home too now—and thought about it. He had stripped to his underwear and sat on the side of the bed to watch her while she undressed, but she had put her gown on over her head before she took off her clothes. Then he said, "Come here," touching the bed beside him. So she sat by him, and he turned down the wick until the lamp went out and put his arms around her. For a long time he kissed her and felt her just as he had done during the past year whenever they had been alone together. But now they didn't have to listen for others or hurry. It seemed that they would go on sitting there forever, knowing they had all the rest of their lives together. This time her body wanted him when he finally pushed her down. And when they had made love and finished, it seemed that that was a part of what would go on forever now too.

Not everything about the day had been satisfactory. She had wanted to go straight to Ral's family's house after breakfast, but he insisted that they face her parents first.

"Mammy'll throw a fit," she predicted. And she braced herself for it. But what she was not prepared for was her mother's bursting into tears and hugging her. All Mammy told Ral was "Take good care of my baby." Pap hugged her, too, and shook hands with Ral.

Annie Bee had gathered up her clothes before she eloped, so she had only to put them into a grass sack. She got the quilts that she had made, and her mother gave her so many other bedclothes, ticks, pillows, and cooking vessels that she and Ral, as well as his horse, were loaded. Her mother hugged her one last time, load and all, and she felt that her own heart was weighting her down. Only Callie Jane was clearly glad to be rid of her and have their room and their parents all to herself.

Ral's sister Molly Lou had been no happier to welcome her than Callie Jane would have been to get her back. After Mr. Henderson shook Ral's hand and Mrs. Henderson hugged Annie Bee and the others congratulated them, Mrs. Henderson said, "Molly Lou, will you be willing to move into Leathie and Lusetta's room?" Molly Lou had lived alone in a little room at the side of the front room since old Mrs. Henderson, Ral's grandmother, had died. Leathie and Lusetta shared the big workroom built across the back of the house.

Molly Lou folded her arms across her chest. "Why do I have to move? Why can't they sleep up in the loft where Ral always has?"

"We can't ask Annie Bee to climb up the ladder; it's not ladylike. And Hoyt's up there too."

"So it's me that has to move. Nobody ever goes out of their way for me."

"Now, Molly Lou, I hope you'll welcome Annie Bee; she is your sister now."

Molly Lou's looks weren't anybody's idea of a welcome. All the time she was moving her clothes into the workroom, she frowned and banged the chests and doors. But Annie Bee didn't care; Molly Lou was always complaining about something anyhow. She could have had her own house if she had stayed in Ridgefield with her own husband the way a wife ought to. And Annie Bee would work Ral around to getting them a place of their own soon. For now, this snug little room would do nicely. But when they had children of their own, they would need their own place.

Thinking of babies, she went to sleep.

II. Fooling Around

In the morning at breakfast, Annie Bee asked Mrs. Henderson what work needed to be done, and the older woman replied, "Leathie and Lusetta need to pick and break the snap beans this morning. Molly Lou and me are dyeing wool; you watch so you'll know how to do it yourself, but it would be a help if you'd leave us in time to fix dinner. The men'll be coming in hungry from the fields, and we need to keep stirring the yarn once we start dyeing it."

"Oh, Ma," Hoyt complained, "you mean we're all going to have to eat bride's cooking? A man needs good victuals to keep him working all day."

"Then you'd better finish those grits and eggs and quit your belly-aching. I'm sure Annie Bee's cooking will be worth as much as your day's work."

The women dyed yarn in the wash house, down by the springhouse. As Mrs. Henderson explained, she and Molly

Lou had scoured the wool before. They had picked rhododendron leaves for green dye, tied them up in an old muslin, and soaked them overnight. Now they were preparing the dye bath. They boiled the leaves in the laundry tub for an hour. Then they added copperas for a mordant. Annie Bee helped to cool the dye bath by dipping it out and pouring it from one kettle to another.

Mrs. Henderson explained all the while about different colors from using other plants and other mordants; Annie Bee was reminded of her own mother's trying to teach her about herbs to use to cure various ailments, but this seemed more interesting. Finally, when the dye bath was cool enough to suit Mrs. Henderson, they wet the yarn and lowered it into the tub. Then they built up the fire and began heating it all over again. Mrs. Henderson said that the slow heating was necessary to keep the wool from shrinking. By then it was time for Annie Bee to leave to start dinner.

She was surprised when Hoyt came into the kitchen not long after she had begun mixing the cornbread. "Reckon your breakfast done give out on you," she said.

"Yeah, well, I thought I'd come get some cooking lessons." Hoyt grinned. He had a big mouth and more tomfoolery in him than the rest of the Hendersons put together. Annie Bee snorted and went on with her work while he pulled out a chair and sat down straddling its back. He settled down to watch her with his chin on his long arms folded across the top of the chair.

"Say, Annie Bee, you're awful brave, I think, to sleep in that old room of Molly Lou's."

"Why? What's wrong with that room? I'm not any braver'n Molly Lou, I reckon; she slept there all by herself."

"Yeah, but the ghosts wouldn't mind a woman by herself there; it's what happens when a man and a woman sleep there together that riles 'em." He grinned again, and she looked down and blushed.

"What ghosts?" she asked.

"Why, ain't you never heard about Old Man Epsom and his daughter and his two sons?"

"No, and I don't want to hear it now if it's some low talk, Hoyt Henderson."

"Aw, Annie Bee, you're a old married woman now. And you really need to know about this if you're going to be staying in the very room that it happened in."

"All right, then, you tell me. I'll see if it's something I can believe or not."

"Oh, you can believe it all right. Paw told me about it. You see, there was this old widow man, Zach Epsom, with two sons and one daughter, name of Susie, and she was the prettiest gal anybody ever saw. But her paw wouldn't let any fellow come near her, and one of her brothers stayed with her all the time to keep anybody from stealing her away. One of them even slept outside her door ever' night.

"But there was this fellow named Andy Scott who saw her at church and took a shine to her and vowed he'd have her, paw and brothers or none. And he was a real good hunter, so he could walk through the woods without stirring a leaf. And he sneaked up to Susie's window one night and climbed in before she knowed he was there.

"Now she was kind of tired of being locked up all the time, and he was a likely looking fellow, so she didn't raise a ruckus, or Andy would've been one dead Scott. But they sat and whispered awhile, and they sparked a little when they heard her brother snoring, and they made up that Andy would come back again sometime. And things being what they are, he come back pretty often, and they did what's pretty natural for a young fellow and gal alone together like that to do, and she got in the family way.

"Well, soon as her paw knowed what had been going on, he got madder'n hornets and vowed he'd get revenge on whoever done it to his daughter. But he didn't know, so he kept quiet and laid a trap for whoever it was. He put one brother at the door, like usual, but him and the other one hid in the cedars on the other side of Susie's window, and they just waited till they saw somebody coming. And Andy sneaked up to the window like usual, but he heard something rustling in the cedars, so quick as lightning he turned around and fired and killed Old Man Epsom and his son both and climbed in the window to Susie, but the other son heard all the racket and busted down the door into Susie's room and shot Andy and her both. And ever' full moon, them four men come back to that room and fight it out all over again."

Annie Bee had stopped her work halfway through Hoyt's story, but when he reached the end, she started slicing tomatoes again. "I don't believe a word you said, Hoyt Henderson. Your pappy built this house himself; your mammy told me so."

"Yeah, but he built it right where the old one was. It burned down. Folks thought he was crazy to live up here nohow. But Paw's not one to be scared of much."

"Well, I'm not either, 'specially some farfetched tale like that."

"All the same, Annie Bee, I'd be scared to sleep in that room. Ain't there a full moon coming tonight?"

"If there is, it's just to shine on loonies like you. Now get on out of here if you want to have any dinner." She twirled the cuptowel into a rope and cracked it on his leg. Howling as though she had crippled him, he hobbled out to the wash house to complain to Molly Lou and his mother.

Annie Bee went on with her work.

That night she did think of Hoyt's story when she looked out at the moonlight on the big cedars at the edge of the woods. There seemed to be white shapes moving there that could be ghosts. She thought about asking Ral whether the story was true, but she didn't want him to think she would believe such foolishness for one minute. So she said nothing about it.

The moon had gone down or been covered by clouds when she awoke, for it was black as pitch. All was quiet, but she felt as though she had been awakened by a sound, though she couldn't remember what it was. She lay listening for another and heard numerous creaks and rustlings, but she hadn't been in the house long enough to know if they were its usual night noises or not.

She had just about decided that nothing was strange when she heard a creak that could only be the bedroom door opening. It was so dark that when she looked straight at the door, she saw nothing; but when she forced herself to look to the side, she saw a ghostly glimmer of white.

Paralyzed, she tried to scream but could make only a squeaking noise. Then Ral sat up and said, "What—?" just as another white shape rushed from the window to clamp a hand over his mouth, while the shape by the door muffled Annie Bee's attempt to cry for help.

It was when she felt the hand over her mouth that she knew that these were no ghosts, but solid flesh and blood. She wished that she could open her mouth enough to bite the covering palm. Hoyt must be one of them; she knew Nate by some unconscious way she would have known him in a crowd of hundreds. Soon from the snickers and whispers she figured out that the third was Joe Conyer, the remaining regular member of Ral's old gang. And of course she knew what they were doing: it was a shivaree. She might have expected it; any new couple was likely to get that dubious welcome to married life. But it made her furious: her own brother and Ral's and a good friend subjecting her to the fear she had known and the teasings she would get from everyone as soon as they heard about it.

They soon made their plan clear. They made Ral dress and climb through the window and marched him outside toward the barn; Annie Bee knew as well as they did that they would take him a few miles on horseback, take off his shoes, and make him walk back, barefoot over gravel.

It had seemed a harmless-enough joke when she had heard of its being played on someone else. Now she shook with rage as she thought about spending the rest of the night alone to remember Hoyt's stupid ghost story and about being teased at breakfast by the family. Ral would arrive home tired, footsore, and out of temper. And everybody around would hear about it by nightfall, for Hoyt would certainly let them all know what had happened. He would get off scot-free.

Or maybe he wouldn't. He'd ride back home and go to bed after they left Ral to walk home. Maybe she could fix up a little welcome for him. She slipped out of bed and went into the big room past his parents' bed. Most likely he had gone out the back door to keep from waking them in case they had slept through the commotion when his crew attacked. She checked the front door; it was chained. But the back door wasn't. Then that's how he would come in.

Next she had to choose her position. She didn't want to mess up Mrs. Henderson's kitchen floor, but the stoop would be all right, and she could hide in the shadow of its roof and the wisteria vine. But she would have to stand up on something; Hoyt was a good foot taller than she was.

Afraid Hoyt would get back before she completed her preparations, she hurried to move a chair to her chosen hiding place, then got a small kettle and went down to the wash house. Mrs. Henderson had directed them to leave the yarn in the laundry tub cooling overnight to make the color deep and true; they would rinse it in the cold water of the spring in the morning. Annie Bee scooped up a kettleful of the dark green dye and walked back up the hill to the back door. There was just enough light to make the shadows visible, and she was startled several times when something in them seemed to move.

When she reached the stoop, she climbed up on the chair and began her wait. It was longer than she had expected. When she thought that her arms would break, she eased the kettle down to rest on the chair between her feet. But she was afraid that she would turn it over, so she bent down to hold the bail until she couldn't stand the ache of her back. Then she would try holding it up awhile again.

Finally she heard hoofbeats coming. Hoyt took his horse to the barn, then came toward the house, singing under his breath. She smiled in anticipation and raised the kettle.

26

She was up first for breakfast the next morning. Mrs. Henderson soon came and took over part of the cooking. Mr. Henderson sat at the table. No one talked except to say "Good morning." When Hoyt came down the ladder to go milk, he greeted them without turning around and went out the back door toward the barn. Molly Lou went down to the wash house to check the yarn; Leathie and Lusetta came in to help with the cooking.

By the time that breakfast was ready, Ral came in and sat down. Mr. Henderson looked at his puffy eyes and drooping shoulders and said, "Reckon a man can't get a good night's sleep when he's took a new wife, but I don't know why he can't leave the rest of the house in peace. What kind of caterwauling around was you doing last night, nohow?"

Ral grinned and said, "Sorry, sir, it's not exactly something I planned."

Mr. Henderson grunted and returned his attention to his biscuits and molasses.

When Hoyt came in the back door, his father put his knife down again. "Lord have mercy. What in tarnation kind of tomfoolery you been up to now, boy?"

Hoyt's grin showed white in a greenish brown face. If he had been a ghost the night before, now he looked like a walking corpse. "Got me a unexpected bath last night, sir. Reckon it'll wash off in a month or two."

Mr. Henderson shook his head in disgust. "Don't know how you all expect to do a decent day's work if you're up playing games all night."

Mrs. Henderson looked at Annie Bee, who couldn't restrain her giggles. "They'll all get their sleep tonight, I warrant."

III. The Doll

It was not hard for Annie Bee to adjust to living at the Hendersons'. When her family had bought part of the old Fowler place from Old Man Nolan and moved to Stone's Creek, she had been six. And six-year-old Leathie had quickly become closer than her own remote older sisters or her pesky younger one. Though they didn't look alike, Annie Bee and Leathie were like twins in size and ways. Leathie had no one near her in age, Hoyt being four years older and Lusetta not born yet. So the two girls spent all the time they could together, more at the Hendersons' than the Cutterfields' since Mammy was often gone helping some woman who was having a baby.

Annie Bee had known Ral first as Leathie's big brother. He had pestered her as well as Leathie until she got to be thirteen. Then he started walking her home from church, taking her to dances, and calling at her home on Sunday afternoons.

Her mother, who had always liked him before, began making rules. She wouldn't even let Annie Bee spend the night with Leathie anymore.

Now Annie Bee could make her own rules.

She and Leathie worked together in the garden or kitchen as they had before. Mrs. Henderson and Molly Lou usually worked with the spinning wheel or loom or knitting needles. Most families bought their cloth or at least their yarn now, but Mrs. Henderson said hers was better, and they had more hands than money, so they might as well use what they had. Annie Bee knew that money was close; having all the children still at home meant more mouths to feed and backs to cover.

The big loom fascinated her, for she had never seen one before. Molly Lou did most of the weaving; she was working on a cotton bedcover in dark blue and red. She followed a pattern punched in holes on a card. It was a beautiful and intricate pattern, with a border around a central design that reversed the colors.

When Annie Bee had time, she came in to watch Molly Lou. At first she had been hesitant, afraid that Molly Lou would drive her away with scathing remarks. But she still came, for she wanted to watch the pattern grow and change as Molly Lou finished the bottom border and began the middle, where the border continued up the two sides.

To her surprise, Molly Lou seemed pleased at her interest. She began explaining to her how to read the punched card and how to use the foot pedals to separate the warp threads, the shuttle to carry the woof through, and the batten to smooth the line.

Emboldened, Annie Bee asked if she could weave a line.

"Well, this isn't a good piece to begin on; it's too fancy. You ought to start on a plain over-and-under line. But I reckon I can help you set the pattern, and then you can throw the shuttle and even up the line."

Even that proved harder than Annie Bee expected; the first time that she threw, the shuttle stopped far short, and she had to work it out and try again—and again—until it came out at the other side. It looked so easy when Molly Lou with her strong wrists threw it. She sat watching without saying anything, and Annie Bee felt clumsier than ever. And when she tried to even the thread, it was too loose, and there were loops. Molly Lou had to straighten it and even it herself.

"When I've got a plain piece on sometime, I'll let you practice on that," Molly Lou told her.

Annie Bee felt like a child put off with a promise and thought that it really wasn't worth the effort. She was just glad that the lesson was over.

Mrs. Henderson did show her how to fit a dress. She was sewing for Lusetta, who was growing like a weed and changing her shape into a woman's as well. And Mrs. Henderson and Leathie taught Annie Bee to crochet. She would have asked Molly Lou to teach her to tat, but as with the weaving, Molly Lou's work with the finer thread looked more complicated than the crochet, and Annie Bee didn't want to risk another failure. She thought that maybe after she had learned to knit, she would try tatting. But maybe Leathie or Mrs. Henderson would teach her.

At night they all sat on the front porch and talked, or Hoyt played the guitar and sang. Sometimes Mr. Walter Spivey would come over to sing and play; he was blind, so one of his nieces or nephews would lead him. Mrs. Henderson sang old songs too sometimes, but the rest of the Hendersons couldn't carry a tune. Annie Bee joined in when they sang church songs.

When it grew colder, they spent the evenings in front of the fire. Mr. Henderson usually went to bed. The others would pop corn on the cook-stove or make molasses candy and tell stories. Ral and Hoyt often played checkers; Ral had played against Annie Bee until he learned that she didn't care whether she won or lost. Then in disgust he refused to play with her.

When Ral wasn't needed on the farm, he worked for Squire Gwaltney breaking horses. The squire's father Len and his mother's father, Old Man Armstrong, had both loved horses, but the squire kept them just to make money. At first he had bred them only to sell, but Acey Jennings had talked him into turning a cornfield into a racing track. And some of them had won money, so the squire's interest had grown. Jennings had raced horses for years, but he didn't have the flat land needed for a track of his own.

Thinking of the Gwaltneys always raised an unpleasant memory in Annie Bee's mind. Haskell Gwaltney had four sisters, all with grand names the teachers used that were shortened by the pupils to more common ones. The youngest, Augusta, or Gussie as she was usually known, was only a couple of years older than Annie Bee. She remembered Gussie's pretty clothes, much nicer than those of the other girls in school.

One day after school when Annie Bee was about ten, Gussie had paid her the unprecedented compliment of telling her that she was coming to visit the Cutterfields that very day. Annie Bee danced ahead of Gussie all the way home, forgetting earlier plans to play with Leathie if her mother would let her. Mammy had welcomed Gussie and given the girls biscuits left over from dinner spread with honey and fresh-churned butter, still soft and pale.

Then Annie Bee had led Gussie to her secret playhouse, a corner of the woodshed shaded by honeysuckle vines and deserted all summer except on wash day. Pap had put a plank top on a section of log to make her a table. There Annie Bee and Ora Mai, her much-loved, much-washed rag doll, had spent uncounted hours mothering and being mothered. Annie Bee brought out of her cigar box all the plates and saucers she had cut out of sycamore bark, the acorn cups used for doll's coffee cups, the discarded thimble worn through like a sieve that she called a vase, all the little bottles she had saved, and the spoons and knives that Pap had whittled out of sticks for her. Mammy had made tiny baskets from acorns too.

The visitor admired the tiny spoons and knives but scorned the rest; she had real china dishes with their own cups and saucers, she informed Annie Bee. "Look at what else I have," she said, and she opened the small pocketbook that she always carried, a thing to be desired in itself. It held a beautiful white handkerchief with store-bought lace all around and pink-and-blue flowers embroidered in one corner, a small folding fan covered with a thin, shiny fabric painted with more pink flowers, a small tortoise-shell comb, a mirror in its own black felt envelope, and a small jar. There was also a little china doll about four inches high with yellow hair and a fluted blue bonnet and dress painted on. Even the buttons on her shoes were raised and painted white to show against the black shoes.

Annie Bee loved her at first sight. "What's her name?" she asked, putting her finger in the space between the arm and tiny waist.

"Artemesia," Gussie said. "She's an old doll of Renie's. But just look at this." She held out the jar toward Annie Bee.

"What is it?"

"Well, silly, you're not like to find out unless you open it."

Inside was something that looked like Rosebud salve, but it was not shiny. "It's rouge, face paint," Gussie explained. "I put it on like this." She set the jar down on the table and, using the mirror, dabbed rouge from her finger onto her cheeks. She looked beautiful to Annie Bee when she was through.

"Can I try it?"

"Yes, I'll let you, but you'd better not let your mother see it. My momma won't even let me wear it, and you're much too young. I got this from my sister Millie. She's over twenty. Here, you'd better let me put it on."

Annie Bee dared not breathe during the rite. When she looked into the mirror, she thought that she was beautiful too.

That was when the goat broke through the fence into the woodlot. He was an adult in size but still an adolescent in behavior. Seeing Annie Bee, his playfellow all his life, he made for her directly, regardless of the dignity and comfort of her guest, who impeded his path. Augusta was knocked aside onto the table, which also collapsed, scattering everything. When Annie Bee, crying as much as the victim, helped her up, she saw a long, red scrape down Gussie's arm, bleeding onto her dirtied, torn skirt. Annie Bee helped the limping, now-wailing guest to her mother, whose ministrations failed to placate Gussie; she insisted on going home at once.

"I'll get your things," Annie Bee said. She ran to the woodshed and gathered Gussie's treasures out of the dust and wood chips, giving her own playthings scant attention as she shoved them back into the cigar box and poked it under the tabletop.

It was two or three days before Annie Bee went back to the playhouse. She set it to rights first, balancing the overturned table again and taking the play dishes out of their cigar box. She wondered what Gussie's china dishes looked like. Maybe Gussie would have invited her over to see them had the goat not come. Now she would never know what they were like.

Walking around the table to seat Ora Mai on her log stool, Annie Bee glimpsed blue among the wood chips: it was Artemesia, dropped in the battle and overlooked in the aftermath. Her bonnet was chipped, and one delicate arm was missing below the elbow. Annie Bee looked until she found the arm; she couldn't find the bonnet chip. She held the arm in its proper place and mourned the marring of the lovely thing.

She would have to give it back; it was Gussie's. But what would Gussie say about the broken arm? Would she think that Annie Bee should pay for it? It was Annie Bee's goat's fault that it had been broken. But Annie Bee had no money. And there was nothing she had that she could give Gussie to repay her for the doll, nothing fine enough that Gussie would want.

And Gussie hadn't even missed it yet.

Maybe she wouldn't miss it. Maybe it didn't mean enough to her to miss.

Maybe it was Annie Bee's now.

But that was wrong. It was the same as stealing to keep something that didn't belong to a body.

But what if it had just got lost? What if Annie Bee hadn't just happened to see it? After all, it could have stayed lost forever among the wood chips and the dirt, gotten tramped down and broken into a million pieces until no one would have known what it was. It would have if she hadn't just happened to see it.

So maybe she was supposed to see it. Maybe it was supposed to be hers. Surely Gussie didn't want it as much as she did.

She shoved it into her pinafore pocket and gathered up the unused dishes and put them away again. She would go back to the house and see if Mammy needed some help.

That night when she took off the pinafore, she remembered Artemesia in the pocket and took her out. Where could she keep her? She couldn't leave her out with Ora Mai where Mammy could see her; Mammy would certainly want to know where she came from. Callie Jane would find her if she hid her in their room. She couldn't take her to school; Gussie would surely see that she had her. The cigar box was not safe from Callie Jane's meddling, although she had her own play-house. Annie Bee would have to find a safer place.

For tonight, she would have to put Artemesia back into the pinafore pocket and hide her before she left for school in the morning. But where? Mammy might find her among the clothes in the chest of drawers. Callie Jane might find her in any other place she could think of.

She could dig a hole and put her in it. But that would be like burying her. Of course, Gussie had kept her in the pocketbook most of the time. Maybe it wouldn't be very different if she was wrapped up in a nice piece of cloth and hidden in a hole.

But then Annie Bee would have to dig her up every time that she wanted to play with her.

The broken arm bothered her too. She needed Mammy's glue that she mended the handles on her cups with. But Annie Bee didn't know where it was or how to get it without Mammy's knowing. She hoped the arm didn't hurt Artemesia too much.

Then she thought of a hiding place: the hollow fence post that the catbird had built a nest in last spring. Because she had taken the empty nest out and looked, she knew that there was a hollow below it big enough to hold Artemesia. She could put something—a wood chip or maybe a scrap of oilcloth or something—over her to keep the rain off. And since the post was behind the big spirea bush, she could take her out and play with her there without being seen. Having solved at least one problem, she settled down to sleep.

Then she remembered that she had not said her prayers.

How could she pray? How did she dare call on God when she was stealing, on purpose and without repentance? Maybe He would strike her dead, there in her own bed, like the firstborn of Egypt when His angel of death passed over the houses of the children of Israel. And then in the morning Mammy would find the doll in her pocket and know that she had sinned. Annie Bee must give the doll back.

But she couldn't give it back tonight. She would wait until tomorrow when she saw Gussie at school. She would tell her most of the truth: that she had found the doll that afternoon where the table had been overturned. The Lord would have to wait until tomorrow night for her to pray.

She was afraid to go to sleep but finally did.

The next day, she carried the doll in her pocket. But Gussie didn't seem to know; she paid her no attention at all. Annie Bee had decided to give it to her at recess. But Leathie and Lida Rae Conyer wanted her to play London Bridge, and she didn't see Gussie at all. So she waited until lunchtime. Again, there seemed no good time to talk to Gussie. Maybe after school she could do it.

But she didn't. Gussie left with her sister Mandy before Annie Bee got outside. She would have had to run after them to catch them. And she didn't know how to tell Gussie with Mandy there.

Again she didn't pray, but she slept better.

All during the church service Sunday morning, she expected to be singled out as a sinner, by the preacher if she were lucky and by God if she were not. But the sermon was on tithing, and nothing in it or the hymns seemed to accuse her. She bowed her head with the others during the prayers and fervently agreed with all the requests for forgiveness. But she made no vows of restoration. That afternoon she put Artemesia in the fence post, covered her with the bottom that had broken out of one of Mammy's fruit jars, and replaced the bird's nest. Every afternoon for the next week, she checked the cache; on Wednesday and Thursday she took Artemesia with Ora Mai to the woodshed for a tea party.

That Sunday was Mammy's birthday. The older children and their husbands and wives, Wilda and Duncan, Sally and Cleavus, Idell and Joe Edward, brought all of their children and enough food for thrashers, as Mammy said. After church they had a picnic. Several of the women were sitting together watching a croquet game and talking when Wilda, the oldest girl, asked Mammy how she had been, and Mammy confessed that all the putting up of food for winter, the sauerkraut and pickles and dried things, had worn her down. She put her arm around Annie Bee and squeezed her. "But this little one has been a real help the last week or two. I can't remember any of you all being so good for so long! She's just been a little angel!"

Wilda said, "Well, I'm glad to hear it. I wish my younguns would help some."

Annie Bee looked down and escaped as soon as she could to take the doll from the fence post.

The next day she gave it to Gussie, explaining that she had found it.

Gussie said, "It's all broken; it's nothing but trash now. I don't want it. Keep it or throw it away."

Of course Annie Bee kept it. She asked Mammy to mend it, and it looked almost as pretty as before. She set it on her corner of the dresser. But she never played with it like Ora Mai again.

IV. A Birth

The rest of the Hendersons had more public memories of the Gwaltneys. Haskell Gwaltney had come calling on Molly Lou before she had run away from home to marry Mr. Elliott, the man from Ridgefield. After that, he hadn't courted anyone else, although he had done a good job marrying off his sisters; of the four, only Gussie was still at home. And he had married them off without destroying the wholeness of the family land. Despite whatever had happened between him and Molly Lou, he didn't seem to blame Ral for his own single lot, but had publicly said more than once that Ral was worth his money as a trainer.

Ral loved the horses for their own sake and would have worked with them for nothing if Gwaltney could have imagined such an attitude and offered him the chance. Ral and Acey watched the horses and talked endlessly about their histories and personalities. Gwaltney asked only about purses, rents, wagers, and stud fees. Annie Bee asked only about wages; she saved Ral's ready cash in a clean sausage sack to use toward a place of their own.

One December evening Ral came home telling about a new sort of horse contest: Brother Manning had come to Gwaltneys' to persuade the squire to give up his racing for the good of his soul and for the sake of his political position. Gwaltney had listened politely, then told the preacher that he always paid his tithes in money from the horses; he promised to give up the racing if the preacher would give up the tithes. Attempts to alter the conditions of the agreement having failed, the preacher left with some frustration and no contract.

But he evidently didn't give up. The next Sunday his sermon was on the wickedness of gambling and the spotless lives needed of those in high places.

Squire Gwaltney intoned "Amen!" with his usual assurance.

A week or two later, Ral reported that the preacher had enlisted the squire's mother, Mrs. Gwaltney, in his cause, pleading her eternal rest as reason enough to guide her son from his wickedness.

Ral's mother looked at his father. "Yes, Rhoda's gotten uncommon Christian in her late years. She needs Len back to give her something to think about besides Heaven."

Ral answered, "Well, if her getting to Heaven depends on the squire losing a dollar or two, she'll find it a narrow way all right."

By January the path had been broadened. Squire Gwaltney gave up the track but not the money; he sold it to Acey Jennings. But the horses still stayed in his barns and grazed in his pastures. Ral speculated that since Acey didn't have enough money to buy even the track outright, the squire probably didn't lose by the deal. Annie Bee supposed that gambling was wrong, but there was nothing wrong with training the horses; she was pleased that Acey had asked Ral to work more often with them. That meant more money for their own place. And since all her Presbyterian upbringing had made her sure that she was one of the elect, it must be

God's will that Ral train the horses to get more money to buy their place.

His parents had already told them that they could move into his grandparents' old house; it stood in a corn bottom on the part of the farm across the creek. But they wouldn't give the place to Ral and Annie Bee or even sell it; they said that it wouldn't be fair to Ral's brother and sisters. That rankled some with Annie Bee, for she had heard that Mr. Henderson had given Clem and Nora, his children by his first wife, the farm they lived on. But Ral would not say anything to his parents about it. Annie Bee knew the Hendersons needed all the land that they had to support their own family, so they wouldn't sell it even if she and Ral had the money. So she resigned herself to looking for some other place to buy. God expects even the elect to look out for themselves.

One cold February day Ral came home from Gwaltney's early and called her as soon as he came through the door. "Get your coat on, Annie Bee, and I'll take you to see something I'll bet you never saw before."

"What're you talking about, Ral? It's freezing out there, and I've got my ironing to finish. I can't just pick up and go whenever you take a notion."

"Old Maude's about to foal, and I just thought you might want to see it." He seemed dampened.

"Well, all right. But I got to finish this bolster case first."

She rode behind him on one of Acey's horses. He trotted to get there before the foal was born, and it wasn't easy to hold on with the jolting pace and the wind determined to blow her skirts up like any hussy's.

The barn was surprisingly warm and light. Acey and Gwaltney, the farrier Gerald Simkins, and a couple of other men, probably Gwaltney's hired men from the looks of their clothes, were standing around in the stable's central alleyway, looking into a large stall with quilted mats tied onto all the walls. Several lanterns were hung on ceiling hooks, and one of the strangers held a lantern up too. It reminded her of the Christmas pageant at the church where some woman acted like Mary while boys in sheets stood around holding walking sticks as though they were shepherds. The men moved aside to give her a closer look. A mare with gray liberally sprinkled through her bay coat was lying on clean straw. She raised her head at the noise of the newcomers. Her eyes looked glazed, as though seeing something past them.

"Well, Missy, we brung you a midwife here," said the man with the lantern. "Don't know as we can call her a granny-woman yet."

"Naw, but her ma is a sure-enough granny-woman: Mrs. Cutterfield, birthed half the babies around," Acey said. "But you better be minding that lady on the ground 'stead of this pretty little one. I'd take care of her myself if her husband warn't here." Acey winked and grinned at her.

She didn't really like him; she never knew how to take his teasing.

As usual, Ral said nothing. She saw that he was watching the mare.

"It's a-coming," he said. The filmy gray bag began to protrude as the mare's body drew up. "That's one."

"What're you counting?" she asked, speaking as softly as she could.

"Her pains. That's two, and the head's out. She's doing fine. A couple more, and it'll be done."

And it was. Ral moved through the stall door and knelt by the foal just as the bag broke; he pulled the torn sides apart. The afterbirth, a bloody, fibrous mass, had come out too.

The mare bit the cord, and the foal jerked its head up and looked from side to side, amazed. "It's a colt," Ral announced.

"Praise be," said Acey. "Though a filly like its dam would be worth a lot too."

"She's been a good brood mare," Gwaltney concurred.

Maude lived up to the praise; she had already begun to nuzzle and clean her scruffy-looking, wet offspring. The colt had continued its jerky movements, as though it didn't know what to do with its bones and muscles when they were set free. Urged by Maude's nudges, it finally stood, collapsed, and stood again, all to the encouragement and exclamations of its audience. Maude had risen too, and the colt found her udder as iron finds a magnet. The mare began eating the bag. That seemed the final curtain for the play, for the group of men began moving away.

Ral spared the horse on the ride home. Annie Bee went over what she had seen in her mind. She asked, "What would have happened if the colt hadn't come out all right?"

"We'd've had to've helped the mare. You got to be careful, though. You can't use a rope or chain, like with a cow. And you can't pull except while she's having a pain."

She had seen kittens and puppies born before. But this was different. She would have to ask Mammy which was more like having a baby.

V. Womantalk

As soon as the weather got warm enough, she went with Ral's mother to see the old homeplace and decide what had to be done to make it livable. They packed a lunch and cleaning equipment to do what they could while they were there. Leathie stayed home to prepare dinner for the family; Molly Lou was weaving as usual.

The house pleased Annie Bee. There were an old orchard and garden beside it and big trees around it. The lilac bushes were as tall as small trees. It looked protected by the hills around it, and the creek was pretty, with rocks and little falls breaking up the flow. The outbuildings looked to be in pretty good shape; some of them had been used all along for storage or for housing animals. The house itself was big, too—bigger than the one they were all living in, though it had only shutters instead of window glass. But so did many other older houses in the community. There were three rooms, all the length of the house: a central kitchen–sitting room and a bedroom on each side.

She asked Mrs. Henderson why they had not moved there themselves.

The older woman looked at her ruefully. "No—I could never live here. It would call to mind too many things I don't want to think on."

Annie Bee hesitated before asking any more; she didn't want to be impertinent. But she did want to know, and she was a woman now, so she asked. "Was it—was it because Mr. Henderson's mother warn't good to you, ma'am?"

Mrs. Henderson laughed. "Oh, no, child, nothing like that. Jake's mother was as good to me as my own mother was, barring the first years we was married, when she thought I warn't good enough for her boy. I come to think as much of her as my own ma; I named Molly Lou for her. No, she was a good woman, and it's not thinking on her that keeps me out of this house. And there's nothing here to keep you from enjoying it."

They had reached the yard by then. An enormous pear tree shaded the back porch, and a beech dominated the front yard. The house needed a lot of work. Moss had grown over all the logs and shingles; the women worried about rot, but at least the logs that they could reach seemed sound. They were of yellow poplar, so termites hadn't touched them. The roof was another matter; it was obviously sagging. Inside they could see watermarks in many places, both where the roof had leaked and where rain had blown in between the logs. The whole roof would have to be replaced, and the walls would have to be rechinked. But the floors were in good shape except for a few boards that had rotted out under bad leaks, and the walls stood foursquare on their high rock foundations. The huge fireplace and the chimney seemed sound too.

Considering the work that would have to be done, it seemed useless to knock down the cobwebs, dust the furniture, and sweep the floors, but they did it anyhow. Annie Bee was happy to see the good cook-stove and well-made furniture—better than her folks had. "Why has all this been left here all these years? Didn't Ral's grandmother live with you all a long time before she died?"

Mrs. Henderson smiled. "Yes, she did—years and years. But she was always funny about that: she wouldn't move her things from here except what she needed. She said long as everything was in order here, she knew things was all right. She said she'd been happiest here, and she wanted to know it was still home if she wanted to come home. And right before she died, she did; she moved back down here when she got sick and died in her own bed."

They laughed together at the strange notion, and after a minute of silent dusting, Mrs. Henderson said to Annie Bee, "She was a good mother-in-law to me, child, and I want to be a good mother-in-law to you. Don't pay any mind to my gruff way; I don't mean anything by it."

Annie Bee looked at her. "Oh, no, ma'am; you've never made me feel bad. I get along better with you than I do with my own mammy."

Mrs. Henderson smiled again. "Well, that's not uncommon. Most girls your age don't like their mas too well. If you'll think on it, you'll probably agree that Leathie likes your ma better'n she likes me."

Annie Bee laughed, thinking of Leathie's exasperation with Mrs. Henderson sometimes when Annie Bee had thought maybe Leathie was the one in the wrong. She wondered if Leathie had ever felt the same way about her own arguments with Mammy. That would be something to ask Leathie about sometime. If she really wanted an answer.

Mrs. Henderson went on. "There's something else about mothers and daughters fighting. It seems to go on just when they've got to separate from each other anyhow. Maybe they have to fight so they can bear to lose each other."

That seemed to Annie Bee to be a new way of looking at people—not for what they do and say but for why, for reasons they don't know themselves, but reasons that make their lives take the shapes they do.

"Is that why Molly Lou come back home after she married Mr. Elliott—because she couldn't lose you?"

Mrs. Henderson looked at Annie Bee. "Yes, I'm afraid that was part of it. Molly Lou and me've always been close. I clung to both my first two babies too hard, and Molly Lou's the one that liked the things I like. But there was something that happened between Molly Lou and Haskell Gwaltney, too. And part of it's Mary. She was always so sickly, and Molly Lou took care of her like she was older instead of younger. So she was a right headstrong young girl when she married. She probably wouldn't have married at all if Mary hadn't upped and married Gavin and left home first. Molly Lou's husband thought he would raise her to suit him, and both of them found out that she was already raised to suit herself."

"Well, at least Ral won't have to worry about me being too headstrong for him already; I reckon that's why he robbed the cradle." She laughed.

Mrs. Henderson opened her lips but put them together again.

Annie Bee went on. "Do you think Leathie will marry Nate?"

"I don't know. Leathie wants other people to make up her mind for her. And maybe she's waiting to see what Nate wants; if he don't want to marry her, she's better off not making him."

"Oh, I think he wants to right enough, or at least, he'd want to if he knew what it was like."

"Maybe so. I reckon we'll all see."

When they were dusting the huge, heavy bedstead in one bedroom, Annie Bee asked, "Is this the bed Ral's grandmammy died in?"

"Yes. She was real impatient toward the end—said she had had to live too long alone already. She said that's what she had learned—that most of living is being alone. Reckon there's some truth in that."

"But you're hardly ever alone."

"No, child, not as you would see. But when you're as old as I am—as old as she was—you'll know you can be alone no matter how many people you're with. Jake's ma warn't by herself neither. No, she didn't mean that. She meant not having anybody to talk to that knows what you mean. Or what you're thinking about or feeling."

"I reckon not many folks've got that."

"Well, she said she had it with Ral's grandpa. I reckon she never found it with nobody else."

"Have you ever had it?"

"No, child, I never have. But it don't bother me the way it did her. Reckon I learned early to keep things to myself. And long as I can get along with myself, seems like I don't feel lonesome. It's not always bad to be alone. You can get to know yourself. And if you're happy with yourself, what others do don't matter much. Reckon I've talked more about myself today with you than with anybody else since she died." She gathered up more quilts to add to the musty stack they were taking home to wash.

Annie Bee was reflecting that she had never really been alone—or wanted to be—when Mrs. Henderson added, "That's the bed Ral was born in, too."

"I thought you said you all never lived here."

"No, we didn't, but there was a flood, and I got caught here when my time come. But that was a long time ago. When are you and Ral going to have babies of your own?"

Annie Bee blushed. "Soon as the good Lord wills it, I reckon."

On their way home Mrs. Henderson showed Annie Bee the Henderson burying ground. "This is Ral's grandparents—Simon and Molly. You may remember seeing her; she died about seven years ago." Annie Bee did recall the white-haired woman who had always carried herself so tall. Leathie had cried when Grandmaw, as she called her, had died.

Mrs. Henderson went on pointing out the graves. "Jeremiah and Sarah were their children that died while they were little, and Saul, Jake's brother, came back here to die before

Ral was born; he had got hurt bad in a logging accident somewhere out west. Over here is where Jake and me picked out to be buried. That there's the three younguns we lost: two before Mary and one after Leathie."

"Didn't Mr. Henderson have a first wife that died?"

"Yes, Jake married Mattie Spivey before I ever knew him, but her family's always been buried in the churchyard in town. They were all strong church people, I reckon."

Annie Bee said nothing but thought maybe they were right. After all, this wasn't consecrated ground. She would have to make Ral see the importance of a proper Christian burial, even if the church in Stone's Creek was just Methodist, not Cumberland Presbyterian.

VI. Married Bliss

The pear tree was just beginning to bloom when Annie Bee and Ral moved into the house beside it. Annie Bee took possession with joy: this was her own kitchen, her own bed that she spread her own sheets on. And it would be a good place for her children to be born and live in until she and Ral could buy a place of their own.

Ral worked some to help his parents, but he also planted some fields just for themselves, too. Together they put out a large garden, and Annie Bee thought that they were like Adam and Eve in Eden.

In their own house Ral seemed younger than when they had lived with his family. He joked and laughed more. He also seemed to boss her around less. Maybe when they weren't with his folks, he didn't have to prove all the time that he was the head of his own household.

One evening after he had come in and washed up for supper, he disappeared. Annie Bee had everything on the table, and she went out onto the back porch calling him, her hands on her hips. She called and waited, called and waited, for five minutes. Finally she walked out into the yard under the pear tree. The petals were falling down on her. She called again. Then all at once the petals came down like a blizzard around her. She looked up, and there was Ral, shaking the tree like a windstorm.

Her irritation turned to laughter, and when he slid down the trunk and kissed her, she decided supper could wait. She felt like a cat arching against him, and his haste echoed her desire. Afterward she felt like a kitten, soft and warm, curled beside him. But she soon got up; they were starved and devoured every crumb left from dinner.

She found some old schoolbooks in the house and tried to get Ral to study with her. But he wouldn't learn from her as Nate had; he said that he had no time for such foolishness. And certainly he was busy, working their own fields and his father's and training horses for Jennings and Gwaltney too. He could often have made more money with the horses had he not been tied down to the farm.

One evening when Acey had sent word that he would like Ral to begin breaking a new filly, Annie Bee suggested that the next day she could do the plowing just that once. Ral and Acey were particularly hopeful for the filly, so Ral agreed. The next morning he hitched up the horse to the plow for her, took the lunch she had packed for him in a lard bucket, and left to go to Gwaltney's.

She plowed only a few furrows before she knew that her dress hampered her work. The skirt got in her way walking, and the bodice was too tight to give her room to control the horse and the plow. She had two choices: to give up on what she had said she would do, or to put on Ral's clothes.

All the way back to the house, she remembered what she

had heard all her life from the pulpit about women who put on pants. They were trying to usurp authority. A woman was not supposed to wear that which pertaineth to a man. But the simple truth was that she could not do a man's job in a woman's clothes. She set her mouth.

First she put Ral's overalls on over her dress and tried to tuck her skirts in. But there was no room, and her bodice would still be too tight. So she took off the dress and shimmy and put on his shirt as well as his overalls. Her shoes were too light to protect her feet from the hard clods, but she could not keep his on, so she had no choice. Last, she donned his hat rather than her sunbonnet; from a distance, anyone would think he was the one working in the field.

That afternoon, she quit and turned the horse loose in time to change and get supper ready. Her feet, legs, and shoulders ached; her hands were blistered. But she had plowed much of what Ral could have covered in the same time. And her body under the heavy skirt felt lighter, as though she had released springs inside herself that had been weighted down before.

Ral came home one day and told her that Acey had said that he could have Maude's next foal. "He said he'd pay me more money if he had it, but he didn't, and he could let me have the foal instead. I'd rather have the foal; a man can get more out of a good horse, mare or stud, than just a little cash."

Annie Bee wondered. "Cash is sure. Will you have to pay to have Maude bred?"

"Not if I breed her to one of Acey's or Gwaltney's studs. Otherwise, I will. There's still some of the old Fowler get around; they was from good lines. But they've not been bred well since. Acey's studs are probably as good as any."

"And they won't cost us anything."

"No, though that's not the main point."

"Maybe not."

"We could get a real good line started maybe, Annie Bee; have horses of our own good as anybody's."

"Maybe so."

For several weeks then he reported to her faithfully all his and Acey's discussions of the merits of various sires and breeding times. Finally they chose the stud and decided that they would breed Maude the next February. That would mean she would foal near the beginning of the next year, and the foal would have an advantage if it proved fast because for racing purposes a horse's age was always figured from the first of the year; it would be as old as it could be for its class if it was born in January or February.

Annie Bee was glad to learn that the subject had been laid to rest, at least for the time being.

Annie Bee liked to be outdoors. She always broke her beans and shucked her corn sitting on the back porch under the pear tree. If she had sewing or mending, she sometimes took it to a beech grove on a hill above the house and sat working in the green light under the wide, sheltering branches.

When she was free of duties, she enjoyed taking long walks through the fields and woods picking berries or flowers. It reminded her of Tarpley, where her family had lived before they moved to Stone's Creek. As a small child, she had often gone with her mother to tend some woman who had just had a baby. On those walks through the fields, her mother taught her the different kinds of grain, oats and barley and wheat, bearded and beardless, and the different trees.

Her mother tried to teach her to be careful, too. Once she had been running ahead when Mammy stopped and called her back. "See what you just stepped over?" she asked. There across the path lay a dark snake that looked an inch thick, its length hidden by the oats on both sides. Annie Bee shivered at the memory.

The flame of butterfly weed in the fields always brought back another memory. When she was eight or nine, she and her mother had gone to take some food to an old lady who lived alone. Across a pasture she had seen the red-orange flowers and had wanted to pick them both coming and going, but Mammy had been in too great a hurry. She had also warned that a bull was in that pasture. But the next day, Annie Bee slipped off from home and went back to get the flowers. She saw the bull, but he was a long way away and paid no attention to her. Mammy had spanked her, but the flowers had glowed in a jar on the table.

Now she filled her own house with flowers, those from her garden as well as wild ones.

She and Ral still saw their old friends at church every Sunday and often at the Saturday-night dances. Ral frequently called the sets at square dances, though he didn't fiddle; his pappy had never held with such foolishness.

She visited with Leathie often, but was not pleased with her and Nate; neither seemed serious-minded enough to settle down. Leathie looked like a schoolgirl with her gray eyes gazing straight at the person she was talking with and her light brown braids set back clear of her face. When Annie Bee asked for the hundredth time why she didn't marry Nate, she smiled before answering. ''I reckon if I told you I don't want to, you wouldn't believe me. You know me better'n that. But I'm in no hurry, Annie Bee. Maybe you and Ral don't have troubles, but heaps of married folk do; look at Molly Lou. And if Nate don't want to yet, I don't want to make him.''

''Then if Nate says he wants to go ahead, you'll marry him?''

''Quick as you can get a preacher,'' she answered.

Actually, Annie Bee and Ral had had at least one real quarrel themselves by then. One Sunday after they had eaten dinner and spent the afternoon at Ral's parents, she had said something about Molly Lou's temper, and Ral had snapped that it was no worse than hers. She insisted that she had always kept her temper, even when he had raved on and on about his mother's cooking. He asked what was wrong with his mother's cooking, she said nothing, but he never said anything good about what *she* cooked, he said maybe there was a good reason for *that,* and they shouted at each other at the same time without hearing what the other was saying. Then he said he would sleep in the other bedroom where he could have a little peace and slammed the door shut. She spent the night judging their words and found him guilty of bad temper, lack of loyalty to his own wife, and insensitive taste buds. She felt a white coldness toward him. In the morning she served his breakfast in icy silence, noting with satisfaction that his eyes were as red as hers. But when he came in from the fields for dinner, he hugged her and said he was sorry, he didn't know what had gotten into him, she said it was all her fault, he said no she had been right and he was wrong, and then they started laughing because they were arguing about apologizing for their argument.

Now although Annie Bee remembered the quarrel, it did not discourage her from working to get her brother married off. The next time he stopped in to visit, she badgered him until he held his hands up above his head in mock fear. "Help! I'm just a poor, defenseless man, Annie Bee! You women gang up on me, and I don't have a dog's chance at a flea convention!"

He wasn't as good-looking as Ral, Annie Bee thought, but he always looked so merry a body couldn't be mad at him even if he was just a big youngun. "Don't you love Leathie?" she demanded.

"Why, sure I do, and marrying her'll make me the happiest fool you ever saw. But getting married's like dying and going to heaven; a man can wait for the pleasure of it." He grinned, and his Cutterfield blue eyes danced as she waved him away in exasperation.

Ral still ran around with his old gang: Nate, Hoyt, and Joe Conyer. Sometimes they all got together at Annie Bee and Ral's house and brought their girls, Leathie with Nate, Bonnie Simms with Joe, and whatever wild thing he was chasing at the time with Hoyt. More often the men went off somewhere by themselves, hunting or fishing or drinking some of the white mule the Conyers made, best in the county, Ral said. Annie Bee suspected that they played cards, and she lectured Ral about the wickedness and the expense.

One night when Ral had gone somewhere with them and she had gone to bed early, she was roused by the clatter of hoofbeats and then talking outside. Pulling her dress on over her gown, she opened the door to find Nate in front of Joe with Ral and Hoyt nowhere in sight.

"Where's Ral?" she demanded.

"Now, Annie Bee, don't get upset. He's going to be all right," Nate said. "There's been a—a accident. Ral got shot, and we took him to the doctor's. We come to get you so you can see him."

"Who done it? Who shot him?"

"Now, Annie Bee, it warn't on purpose. We was just fooling around, and Joe had a new gun, and he was showing it off, and it just sort of went off accidental-like."

"I might've knowed it would be you, Joe Conyer, ain't got the sense you was borned with, stark-raving mad, and the rest of you drunken hooligans got no sense neither."

Joe stepped farther behind Nate. "I'm sorry, Annie Bee, just as sorry's I can be, but I didn't mean no harm, honest. I wouldn't hurt Ral on purpose no more'n my own brother."

Nate caught Annie Bee by the wrists just as she was about to fly at Joe. "Come on now, Annie Bee, you're not doing Ral any good here. Get your shoes on, and let's go to the doctor's. You'll see; he's not hurt bad."

Ral looked white as a sheet except for his dark eyes and

hair and the blood all over his head and shirt. She grew weak-kneed when she realized that the bullet that creased his scalp would have furrowed his brain if it had been just a little lower. She wondered about Nate's account of the shooting; she knew that Ral and Joe Conyer both had quick tempers, and they had fought each other with fists more than once during the years of their friendship. She would have to see that Ral quit running with such dangerous company.

Dr. Abbott gave her directions on caring for the wound while he finished bandaging it. "If you have any trouble, let me know. But I reckon Jessie Cutterfield's gal ought to be able to take care of a little scratch like this." His words made her feel better about the wound.

Nate and Hoyt, who had stayed with Ral at the doctor's, took them home. Joe Conyer seemed to have left earlier.

She didn't have any trouble taking care of Ral except that he worried her to death by not staying in bed and insisting on doing more than she thought he ought to. He was well enough by Sunday to go to church, and she felt great thankfulness as she sat beside him and prayed, his white bandage all she could see when she closed her eyes. *Lord, thank you for preserving him for me. He's everything to me.* That didn't seem quite right to her. After a moment, she added, *Lord, don't let me love him too much.* She wouldn't look at him again for a while; she didn't want him to see the fever of her love burning in her eyes.

Book Two

What a Dusty Answer
1914 to 1918

I. Offspring

Ral and Annie Bee had been married for almost a year, and there was still no sign of a child coming. Month after month she was disappointed, then angry, to know that she still was not pregnant. She prayed for a child every morning and night, although she sometimes feared that her very persistence would annoy God and make him withhold it.

One warm June night, as Ral was calling the sets at a square dance, she sat talking with Mary and Gavin. Gavin asked Mary to dance, but she didn't feel well enough and suggested that he and Annie Bee dance together. Annie Bee hesitated, then said, "No, I shouldn't."

Mary said, "Why not, child? You're not in the family way, are you?"

"No, that's the trouble. Ral and I want to have a baby, but we just don't seem to."

"What does that have to do with not dancing?" Gavin asked.

"Well, you know a lot of people think it's not right to dance, 'specially with another woman's husband."

He laughed. "Now, Annie, I'm too old for folks to think a pretty young thing like you would stoop to sin with me. Besides, we've been in each others' families so long we're like brother and sister."

"What folks think is not really what bothers me. I just wondered myself if it's right, and if God would keep me from having a baby for doing it."

Gavin grinned. "It don't seem like God always gives out babies as rewards for goodness."

They laughed, and then Mary said, "Annie Bee, do you think that because I'm not well enough to have a child, God is punishing me?"

Annie Bee said, "Oh, of course not, Mary. I'd never think that. You're as close to a saint as there is here on earth."

"Well, I don't know about that." Gavin grinned at Mary, then looked soberly at Annie Bee. "But sometimes we have to choose what we want most, and I want Mary more than a child. Sometimes we don't have any choice at all, and we just have to make the best of it. But I don't think we can blame God for not giving us everything we want."

Mary added, "And sometimes we just have to wait. Maybe God's telling you to go ahead and have a good time before you lose your figure and have to spend all your time whipping younguns."

They laughed, and Annie Bee said, "If you still want to, Mr. O'Neill, I'd be obliged to you for a dance before I get too old to enjoy it."

They danced till Gavin pleaded his gray hairs and sore feet. As they were walking back to Mary, he told her, "I wish you and Ral luck in having a baby, Annie. If Mary was strong enough, nothing would make us happier."

"I'm sorry, Gavin."

"You'll just have to let us play with yours when you have it. And when it's full of devilment, we can send it back home to you."

62

It was Leathie who told her about Cardui. "Mrs. Arla Simms says she never would've had any babies if she hadn't've took it. Reckon she's got enough now." Mrs. Simms's five, mostly less than two years apart, were notorious for mischief and pestering.

"Maybe it's tampering with the will of the Lord to take medicine for suchlike. If He wanted me to have younguns, He'd give them to me."

"Well, 'The Lord helps those that help themselves,' and I reckon He won't mind if you do a little to help yourself."

So Annie Bee took some money from one of her sausage sacks and went to Nolan's store. Dewey Shakelford, who had run it since Nolan died, grinned when she asked for the medicine, but she pretended not to notice. At home she read everything on the label and unscrewed the top and smelled it, but put it in the back of the safe without taking any. After all, Leathie was a Methodist, and they valued the will of God less than the will of men. Everybody knew that Methodists weren't much of anything; they didn't argue about predestination or the millenium or any of the other important things. She thought about taking the medicine back to Shackelford and asking for her money, but the memory of his grin prevented her.

The next day she took it out again, poured a spoonful, and swallowed it before she had time to change her mind. It was not bad: mildly medicinal but not bitter.

She was halfway through the third bottle when she knew that she didn't need to take any more.

Late the next February, Ral had Maude bred to his favorite stallion from Acey's stables, Jennings's Prospects, known usually as Prosp. Annie Bee began to hope that his get would bring prosperity to them. She felt closer to the expectant mare because of her own pregnancy, and after Ral brought Maude to graze at their place, she would go with him sometimes when he called the mare up for extra hay. Maude learned to nuzzle around Annie Bee's apron pocket for an apple or carrot.

Maude also learned to stretch her neck over the chicken-yard fence and knock the lid off the barrel of corn. When Annie Bee caught her at it, she was incensed that her chicken feed was being pilfered. Ral was upset because he didn't know how much Maude had eaten and he was afraid her diet was too rich. But when she didn't founder, he was relieved.

Clara was born that June. A few weeks before the baby was due, Annie Bee's mother came to stay with Ral and Annie Bee to do the heavy work, and she spent the time teaching Annie Bee how to take care of a little one and what remedies she might need for the baby's ills. When Callie Jane was little, Annie Bee hadn't been old enough to learn how to take care of her.

What their mother didn't teach her was how to prepare for the birth itself. She had two days of labor and was worn out before the delivery; she thought when the pain was greatest that she would rather die than endure it.

But she had never felt such joy as she did when her mother laid Clara in her arms the first time. The baby was just as she had wanted her to be. Even her red hair seemed right and beautiful. Clearly God had meant for her to have this child.

Mrs. Henderson walked over every day to play with the baby and took her home with her as often as she could, although she herself had been ill since the spring. Even the silent Mr. Henderson would rock Clara for hours and, when she got big enough to sit up, trot her on his foot. She was their first grandchild. Ral's brother and sisters made over her too, even Molly Lou. Nate teased Leathie that the only reason she wanted to marry him was to have a baby of her own.

Annie Bee felt closer to her own mother now. Mrs. Cutter-field came to see them whenever she could, bringing toys and herbs for teas. Often, as the two were sitting watching the baby play with a ball while they stitched long dresses for her, Mrs. Cutterfield would start telling Annie Bee about things she had done or said as a child. Once when she had been about five, they had all gone to a brush-arbor meeting where the preacher had passed his hat to collect the offering. Annie Bee had gravely taken the hat from the man next to her, said ''Thank you,'' and started for home.

They laughed, and Annie Bee said, ''I'd probably take a willow switch to a youngun of mine for suchlike.''

''Well, that's probably just what I done to you, child. But every time I switched you didn't mean I wanted to. You'll learn that soon enough when little missy there gets a little older. My pappy always said true: 'You don't pay for your raising till you raise one of your own.' ''

''And you don't know how your mammy loved you till you love one of your own.'' Saying the words, Annie Bee felt shy. But they were true. She looked up to see tears in her mother's eyes, and they embraced each other.

Caring for the baby and welcoming the company gave Annie Bee little time for her house and garden, much less doing things with Ral anymore. He played with the baby himself whenever she was awake and he was home, but he also seemed aggrieved that Annie Bee had less attention for his interests. He kept her fully apprised of Maude's condition. He was jubilant when an examination by the farrier, Gerald Simkins, confirmed that she was indeed pregnant, but he had fretted over a month after he discovered that the mare had been eating fescue, for it was supposed to harm the development of the bag. Certainly, though, Maude was generally healthy, he reassured Annie Bee.

Mary and Gavin were often among Clara's visitors too, or they asked Ral and Annie Bee to visit. Annie Bee remembered Gavin's regret that they couldn't have their own child and was glad that she could give them one to play with. She felt as if she gave happiness to the world by sharing Clara.

That did not make her want to have more babies. She did not want to go through labor again, and Clara satisfied her desire for a child to love. Indeed, now she hoped as fervently not to become pregnant as she had wanted to have a child before. She remembered that Gavin had implied that he and Mary had chosen not to have children, and she wondered if they knew a way to choose. Once when the men were outside together, she asked Mary about it, and Mary told her how.

Telling Ral was not easy. She put it off several times, but each time they made love, she feared the consequences and resolved again to open the subject. She prayed every day for God to give her the strength to talk with Ral about it.

Finally one night after supper she brought him the Bible. "I'd be obliged if you'd read this for me." She showed him the thirty-eighth chapter of Genesis.

"You can read better'n me." He looked up, bewildered.

"I've done read it."

He made a face but settled down to figuring out the words. He spelled out a few for her to decipher, but finally finished. "Well, I've done it. Now why did you want me to?"

"Because I don't want any more babies."

He tossed his heavy black hair back out of his eyes. He looked boyish. "Why? Don't you love Clara?"

"It's not that; you know it's not. And it's not that I don't want you either." She looked down. "But I don't want to go through birthing another one."

He looked away. "I know it was hard for you. I don't want to make you have to either." He looked back. "But I always thought we'd have a lot of younguns playing around."

"One's enough for me."

"What's all that got to do with Judah and Tamar, anyhow?"

"Well, she wanted a baby, and she finally got one by tricking Judah, and I reckon that was all right with the Lord because Judah was the one wrong because he didn't give her

66

to his youngest son. But before that, when Judah gave her to Onan, that's what I wanted you to see the most."

"What about it?"

She took a deep breath. "Well, he didn't want to give her a baby, and it tells what he did so she wouldn't get one."

He applied himself again to the passage. When he had read it, he looked up at her, closed the book, laid it on the table, and stalked out of the house, slamming the door.

For a while he held himself away from her in bed and avoided her when he could during the day. That was all right with her; she bided her time and treated him just the same as always. The night came when he reached out for her. "You tired of fighting?" he asked.

"That depends on how you've made up your mind."

"Me? It's you that's got to change your mind."

"I already told you. I'm not going to change my mind."

He sat up in bed and yelled: "*Aaaaaaah!* It's not fair, woman!"

"What's fair about it if I have another one? You going to birth it? I'm not asking you to live and not . . . do anything. I wouldn't like that either. But you could give up some to keep me from having to bear another one."

Reason or desperation finally held sway, and Ral surrendered. Eventually the new system became routine, though there were still skirmishes enough to show that she had won a battle, not a war. But she was satisfied.

The weather had been too dry for good crops for two years, so everyone was glad to see 1916 begin with rains. Every day during January, Ral would slosh out to the barn to check the stock, mainly Maude. She was due to foal in late January or early February, and he worried that she hadn't seemed to be putting on much more weight in the last weeks. February came and went with no foal, and he became anxious but kept saying that she was an older mare, and they were often as much as a month late bearing. By the middle of March he and Acey had decided that another examination by the farrier was necessary.

When Simkins, Acey, and his usual hangers-on came, Annie Bee served them coffee and gingerbread; she had nothing pressing since Clara was asleep, so she fiddled with her sewing while waiting for them to return from the barn. Ral came in alone, his face making it clear that the news was not good. "She's resorbed the foal," he said.

"What does that mean?"

"Well, it probably means something was wrong with it, and instead of just losing it, her body sort of soaked it up."

"You mean she really wasn't bred?"

"No. She was bred all right, and she was with foal all right, but at some point the foal stopped living, and what would have been the foal and the bag and all just came apart, and what was left went back into her body."

"I never heard of such a thing." She was indignant. "You gave her extra food and everything. And paid the farrier."

"I reckon it's for the best. If the foal was born with something wrong with it, it would have just been to shoot anyhow. Leastways this way Maude builds up her strength."

"I don't see how it could happen. I never heard of a woman resorp—resorbing a baby. It seems like it's against nature."

"No, it's nature all right. I don't know if women do or not, but I've heard of it before with horses. Other animals do it sometimes, too. It's for the good of the mother, I reckon."

"Much good it can do us. If she resorbed this one, she'd probably resorb the next one. So we're just out all we've put in her." She paused. "I don't suppose Acey would pay us back what we're out."

"Now, Annie Bee, be reasonable. Why should he? He give us the chance to have the foal; it's just our bad luck it didn't work out. Otherwise, it would have been his bad luck."

"Well, it just don't seem fair."

Ral shrugged and left, heading toward the barn again.

II. Poor Relations

After the drought years, the weather was giving them too much of a good thing; it rained so much that even by May the farmers could not plow the ground to get the seeds in. Money and tempers were short.

When Hoyt told his family that he was going to marry Trubie Escue and that she was already pregnant, his father exploded and refused to let them live in his house. Ral stood by his brother and offered them his own home, much to Annie Bee's chagrin.

Trubie Escue was just the sort of light woman that Annie Bee couldn't abide. She wore her skirts short enough to let her legs show above her shoe tops. Even her name was foreign-sounding; folks said her grandfather couldn't speak proper English when he moved to Stone's Creek. She looked sort of foreign with her dark curly hair, worn unbraided, and her narrow nose and long chin. It was certain that she painted her face. It was rumored that she stuffed her bosom. And Annie Bee with her own eyes had seen her at the last election-day rally sit right on Hoyt's lap.

She behaved the same way after she and Hoyt moved into the extra room—running to greet Hoyt with a long kiss when he came home from the fields, sitting on his lap and sparking when they all sat together in the evening. Annie Bee as a sober matron was offended and complained about Trubie to Ral whenever they were alone. "She ought not treat him that way right in front of everybody."

Ral grinned. "Hoyt don't seem to mind."

"Well, that's sure God's truth."

She couldn't do anything about Trubie's light ways, but she could about her laziness. There was no sleeping after sunup in Annie Bee's house. And she saw to it that Trubie did her share of the chores: laundry, cooking, housekeeping, and gardening. She didn't ask Trubie to care for Clara, who was walking and getting into anything she could find; her mother wanted no influence from this new aunt.

Of all the tasks, Trubie seemed most ready to help put dinner on the table, and when Annie Bee realized why, her righteous wrath knew no bounds. Trubie was placing the food so that she and Hoyt always got first choice. If there was meat, they took the biggest pieces; if there was chicken, one of them got the pully bone. If Trubie gathered apples for them to eat, the bruised ones went to Ral or Annie Bee. Annie Bee made sure that changed too.

Perhaps worst of all was Trubie's sweet-talk. She was always running on about how grateful they were to her and Ral and how since she never had a sister, she was so glad to have Annie Bee now. Trubie was a year younger than Annie Bee, and Leathie and she had always despised Trubie when they were in school together. Leathie was the only sister Annie Bee acknowledged except her own blood kin. She could think of no suitable way to stop Trubie's protestations of affection, but she certainly had no desire to repay them. She prayed every night that she would soon be rid of Trubie and her husband.

Sometimes, just to get away from Trubie at first and later because she wanted to, she would go out into the fields and woods with her mother to gather herbs for cures and ginseng to sell. One day, her mother asked her to go with her to see Mildred Trapps, who had just had a baby, and Annie Bee asked Leathie to watch Clara and went. It was the woman's first child, and she asked Mammy some of the same questions that Annie Bee had asked. Little Wilbert had just had croup, and Annie Bee told Mrs. Trapps about Clara's croup. Mrs. Trapps asked her to come back and bring Clara, and Annie Bee decided that she would.

After that, she went with her mother almost every week to visit some woman expecting a baby or caring for a new one. Once Mammy sent Callie Jane to fetch Annie Bee for a delivery; Gavin's uncle Campbell O'Neill's daughter-in-law Josie was having a hard time, and the doctor wasn't at home. Annie Bee relieved her mother while she slept and Josie's mother-in-law minded the couple's other children. She sat and held Josie's hand and bathed the sweat off her face. Josie would look at Annie Bee's face and grip her hand, and both of them knew that they were as alive as they would ever be and that they were part of something beyond their lives. When Josie's little boy was born, Annie Bee felt almost as happy as when Clara came.

She understood why her mother had been a midwife all those years; it wasn't because of the two dollars or the eggs she was paid, but because of the sureness inside herself that she was part of the pain and joy that was coming to the women she touched. On their way home, Annie Bee asked her mother to let her help with deliveries whenever she could.

"I'll be glad of the help and the company," Mammy said. "None of my other younguns ever wanted to do this, but you seem to have a bent for it."

"Yes'm. Reckon I got it from you."

"Reckon so. I'm right glad; I worry sometimes what folks'll do when I'm gone."

"Oh, Mammy, you're young yet. But I'd like to learn so I can do something for other people."

"Well, that's good too. I'll let you know when you can help."

And she did; Annie Bee became accustomed to leaving Clara with Callie Jane or Leathie or one of Ral's other sisters. His mother was still not well. Occasionally Annie Bee even took the growing child with her. The women she helped became part of Annie Bee now as surely as her own family, and she knew that they would be even if she never saw them again.

Annie Bee didn't leave Clara with Trubie, who would by the end of the year have her own child to keep and who showed no special eagerness to practice on her niece. Her pregnancy swelled her figure until her clothes were too tight, and Mrs. Henderson made her some loose dresses.

Every time Ral looked at her, he frowned. Annie Bee knew that it wasn't because he wanted Trubie and Hoyt out of the house as she did; he wanted a son.

Almost every night he threw it up to her: his younger brother might present a grandson to the family before he did. And it was all her fault. It was her duty to her husband to give him sons. How else was he to have help farming? She had her daughter; he ought to have a son. And a man needed a son anyhow, to carry on the family name. If she were a good wife, she would give him that. Would have already given him that.

Annie Bee repeated all the arguments she had used before to talk him into not having more children. But she knew that he was not really listening. Sometimes he merely argued against their treaty; sometimes he broke it.

Annie Bee prayed that she would not become pregnant again.

Thinking of the whole problem gave Annie Bee a fierce energy as she plucked the geese one hot August day. She was trying to get enough feathers that summer to make a new featherbed—not for Hoyt and Trubie, she resolved—and she had been plucking the geese's breasts every six weeks since the weather got warm enough. By now they were hard to catch and hard to hold, but she had learned to trap them in a corner and pop a grass sack over their long necks, tuck them under one arm with their heads at her back, and pluck. Now she plucked as though it were Ral's hair she were pulling out.

She reviewed her grievances: the pain she would have to undergo if she became pregnant and the things they all would have to give up if they had a houseful of children.

That was the trouble with the Hendersons now; they didn't have enough land for all their offspring. Aside from Clem and Nora, whose farm evidently wouldn't be shared by the rest, and Mary, who had a good farm Gavin had bought, there were still Ral, Molly Lou, Hoyt, Leathie, and Lusetta. It was just as well those other three babies up in the cedar glade hadn't lived.

She was saving so that she and Ral and Clara would not face such problems. And that was one of the reasons she didn't want more children too. Couldn't Ral see that? She gave the goose a final swift pull and tossed her, honking, back toward the rest.

She got her answer in November; Ral might have his son the next July. She resolved not to tell him for as long as she could. But there was no point in warring anymore. So the next time he importuned her, she answered, "It don't matter. It's too late." She turned her face away from his kiss, but in his joy he didn't seem to notice.

With Annie Bee's help, Jessie Cutterfield delivered Trubie's son in early December. She charged no fee since it would have come out of her daughter's savings. Trubie talked Hoyt into naming the boy Jacob for his father, and his presence in the Henderson family cradle in front of her own fire determined Annie Bee to get him and his parents out of her house as soon as possible.

Mrs. Henderson was eager to help her. She had gotten sicker during the year and was sure that she was going to die; her one wish was to reconcile her husband and Hoyt before her death. Annie Bee suggested that they have Christmas dinner at her house because Mrs. Henderson wasn't well enough to prepare it, and although both of them knew that Molly Lou and Leathie could do all the cooking needed, Mrs. Henderson agreed since it was a way to get Hoyt and his father together.

Indeed, Leathie helped Annie Bee cook and clean every day for a week before the dinner. Trubie was no help; she still stayed in bed most of the time. But she got up and dressed in her best the morning of the dinner. She didn't greet the family when they first arrived, but as soon as everyone had settled down, she made her entrance carrying little Jacob. It was to Mr. Henderson that she took him first. "I want you to see your first grandson, sir."

Ral's father was suitably impressed, and Annie Bee didn't know whether to applaud Trubie's skill in furthering a project they both wanted or to hate her for the dark mood descending on Ral. She didn't have much time to wonder; she was too busy getting the food on the table.

After dinner was finally over, she sat and listened and watched for a while. She had not had leisure before to see

Clara's delight in the first Christmas she was old enough to enjoy. Her favorite gift was a doll bed made by her Uncle Gavin, who did as much carpentry as farming. The tiny beechwood posts were turned like those on a big bed, and Clara insisted that Annie Bee at once find something to make bedding for it so she could install in it the rag doll Mrs. Henderson had made. Then Clara announced that she would rock the doll to sleep "just like Aunt Tubie."

Annie Bee said, "Next summer we'll have a new real baby of our own to rock."

Those who heard the announcement congratulated her and Ral, and the rest asked what they had missed, and soon Annie Bee was basking in quite satisfactory attention herself. She didn't even mind that Trubie again avoided doing any share of the dishes by taking the baby into her and Hoyt's room to nurse at just the right time.

During the afternoon, Ral, Gavin, and Hoyt pitched horseshoes in the mild sun and Mr. Henderson dozed by the fire. Sitting at the table, Mary told the women that she and Gavin had decided to sell their farm and move to the city. Crops had been so bad for the last three years that Gavin made little from farming and the farmers around couldn't afford to pay him for his carpentry. He also wanted to take her to a place where there were more doctors. They had picked out a new town that was growing at Hadley's Bend just outside Nashville, near President Jackson's homeplace. Property there was not so high as in the city, but it was a growing town, so a carpenter could find plenty of work. Some people called it Jacksonville, and some called it Old Hickory after Jackson's nickname.

Seeing Mary beside her mother made Annie Bee think how much they looked alike except for the colors of their eyes and Mary's height. Annie Bee had already noticed the yellow cast of Mary's skin; she looked like a tallow candle burning down with the flame in her eyes. That day both mother and daughter looked as though they were marked for death.

Trubie came back into the main room not long after Mr. Henderson woke up from his nap and spent the rest of the afternoon wooing him like a beau. Her voice trilled above the hum of the conversation like bird-notes. By the time the elder Hendersons left, she and Hoyt had his father's invitation to live in his home. Hoyt's mother and Annie Bee exchanged glances; their plan had worked.

After Ral and she were in their bedroom, Annie Bee told Ral Mary's news. He was sleepy, so she didn't tell him what she was planning now. Anyhow, she wanted to think about it a little more first.

She wanted to buy Gavin and Mary's farm.

She remembered when they had bought it at the county sale after Nolan died. He had quit paying taxes on the land he hadn't sold when he decided that he wouldn't live long enough for the county to take it away from him if he didn't. Actually, he had lived for quite a long time after that, but the squire hadn't let the county prosecute him. So after he died, his hundreds of acres had been split up and sold with his store for taxes on the courthouse steps in Ridgefield. Some merchant from Ridgefield had bought the store, and the land had gone in twenty- to thirty-acre tracts to many people. A nephew named Wilson, who had come all the way from Texas to collect an inheritance, was upset, but that wouldn't have bothered Nolan. And the nephew did get some money, although everyone suspected that Nolan had buried more somewhere. That fruitless rumor had fueled enthusiasm in bidding at the auction, but Gavin and Mary had still gotten a pretty piece of land for a good price, and since they were family, they might sell it to Ral and her without full cash payment. She had a good bit saved in her sausage sacks; they knew she and Ral would honor their debts. She thought with pleasure of the wooden cupboards that Gavin had built for Mary's kitchen and of the rich green that they had painted the front room just that year. She would get Ral to make them some nice furniture, and they would take some of the good pieces of furniture that his grandfather had made—surely his parents would give him that much. They would buy some pretty pieces like the ruffled lampshades she had seen in Ridgefield once. Maybe they could even buy a mohair-upholstered sofa and chairs someday. And she would make pretty curtains and crochet scarves for the chairs and embroider scarves for the tables.

Feeling satisfied about her new plan and about getting rid of Trubie and her family, she drifted into memories about old Mr. Nolan himself. It had been eight or nine Christmases ago that she had gone with her mother to take him a jam cake and a jug of boiled custard. She had asked if he was family.

"No, he's just a old man that won't have no Christmas if nobody takes it to him."

"Why? Is he poor?"

Her mother had laughed. "He's got more money'n we'll ever see, child. No, he's just a old miser that loves his money more'n hisself."

It was hard to believe when she saw him that he wasn't poor. His clothes were filthy and so threadbare that they couldn't have survived a washing. He lived in a tenant house on the old Fowler place, just a stone's throw from the chimneys and rubble that marked where the old Fowler sisters had burned down their big house and themselves in it. Nolan's house was covered with clapboards and looked finer to Annie Bee than the dressed logs on most houses around, but the wood had warped, the nails had sprung out, and many boards stuck out from the logs underneath at crazy angles. The porch steps were broken, so when he invited them in, he had to lift her up and give her mother a hand.

The inside was as dim as a cave. The floor had rotted and sagged and even broken through to the ground in some places. One corner held a bed built into the wall bearing a lumpy-looking tick. The only other furniture was a trunk, a table covered with dirty dishes and scraps, and a ladder-back chair with splintery oak splits on the seat. There were stacks of books everywhere, leaned against each other to keep them from sliding down the uneven floorboards.

The room smelled; it was musty like a cave, but it also smelled of rotten food and the old man's unwashed body. She was glad that they didn't stay long.

Most peculiar of all was what Squire Gwaltney finally revealed about Nolan's money after the sale. It seemed that for years he had been sending a good bit of it to some Catholic orphanage in Louisiana, where he grew up, although everybody had thought he hated Catholics, and the rest had gone to educate young men and even women—sending them to college. A schoolteacher somewhere that he knew told him about students that he helped. He had spent no telling how much money on that. That, and all the books that had mildewed in his house, which wasn't fit to be a good stable.

Now, warm with her new featherbed below and another above, she thought how differently she and Ral would live when they bought Mary and Gavin's place. She prayed, *Oh, Lord, let us have a nice place of our very own.*

When she told Ral what she wanted, he looked away from her toward the door. "We can't. We don't have any money."

"What do you mean? 'Course we got money. I've been saving it ever since we got married. I've got three sacks and more'n half another saved."

"We don't have it no more. Hoyt had some debts, and he asked me for a loan, and I give it to him—all but twenty dollars."

Without a word Annie Bee went to her hiding place in the old quilt chest to see for herself that her hoard was gone. As she looked at the one limp sack left, she heard Ral close the back door. Then she cried.

As soon as it was warm enough to take little Jacob out, Trubie and Hoyt moved to his parents'. Finding her best sheets missing after they left seemed a small price to Annie Bee for getting them out of her sight.

III. War and Death

That spring on Ral's birthday, President Wilson asked the Congress to declare war on Germany, and a few days later it did. The men talked about the war all the time, but Annie Bee paid no more attention than she had to the talk of war in Europe since the first year she and Ral were married. She regretted not having money to buy war bonds; they seemed a safer investment than trusting her money to Barrault's bank in Ridgefield, and they would have been safe from Ral's generosity too.

More important to her was Mrs. Henderson's illness. Dr. Abbott had told them that she had cancer of the womb and that there was nothing they could do for her but keep her easy. She was bedfast most of the time.

Trubie and Annie Bee tended her during the day; the family all took turns sitting up with her at night, and the neighbors helped. Clem and Nora, Mr. Henderson's children by his first wife, came to sit up with her too, although Clem and his father hadn't spoken to each other for years. Clem, who seemed to Annie Bee as big as she imagined an ox to be, didn't have much to say to anybody. Nora said "Ma Julie," as she called her, was the only mother that she remembered.

Mammy and Callie Jane came when they could to help care for Mrs. Henderson. Of course, Annie Bee could no longer go with her mother to help at deliveries, so she looked forward to Mammy's visits.

Leathie and Lusetta did the cooking, housework, and gardening; Molly Lou alone did the shearing, carding, dyeing, spinning, weaving, and knitting that she had done for years with her mother. Ral and Hoyt had to do more of their father's work, too; he had grown feeble, as though his years had come down upon him all at once with his younger wife's illness.

The one effect of the war on Annie Bee was that Nate soon decided to join the army. He sat in her kitchen and told her, his hands restless as always, his eyes looking out the window toward some distant shore in his mind. "After all, Tennessee ain't called the Volunteer State for nothing. I might as well go do some good over there as sit around here and wait to be called up."

His choice made him and Leathie decide at long last to get married. Annie Bee, who had given up on getting them properly settled down, was jubilant, as happy as Leathie. Indeed, she accused Leathie of not showing proper joy.

"Well, he'll have to leave for camp right after the wedding. There won't be time for a honeymoon, much less a real marriage. And when he goes off, he might . . . he might not come back."

"But it won't happen that way for you. It's bound to work out all right."

"So you think we're some of the elect? Remember, Annie

82

Bee, I'm not even a Presbyterian; I'm one of those godless Methodists you're always talking about."

Annie Bee blushed. "Oh, Leathie, you know I don't mean you and the rest of your family when I'm talking religion. And anyway, you may not be a Presbyterian, but Nate is."

Leathie laughed. "Well, thank goodness, I'll be saved by the power of Saint Nathaniel!"

Then Annie Bee had to laugh too at the idea that her mischievous brother's godliness was going to save anybody.

Leathie and Nate had a quiet wedding at her parents' with Ral and Annie Bee standing up for them.

Gavin and Mary had bought a Model T Ford automobile, and they drove it home for the wedding. At least, they drove it as far as the junction of the Hendersons' wagon road and the main road to Stone's Creek; Gavin would not risk his axles on the deep ruts of the wagon road.

Mary looked better; she had been seeing a doctor whose medicine had helped her. He had told her that ever since she was born, her heart had not been right and that her other organs were damaged because the bad heart had made them work harder. But proper medicine and caution could prolong her life and increase her strength. Annie Bee asked her when they were alone if the doctor thought she could have a baby, and she said no; Annie Bee gave her a sympathetic hug.

Mrs. Henderson sat up for the wedding and even moved to the table for dinner. She seemed as excited about Mary's improvement as about Leathie's marriage. "Gavin, thank you for taking good care of my girl. I hope my boys are as good to their wives as you've been to Mary."

Annie Bee noticed that she didn't say anything about Nate. But of course he wasn't tried yet to praise, and he wasn't Mrs. Henderson's son to admonish.

After dinner Mrs. Henderson was exhausted, so Annie Bee and Leathie put her back to bed. The day was hot for May, and when the dishes had been washed and put up, the women went outside to join the men, who were sitting on the porch or steps. Annie Bee spread a quilt on the grass, and Gavin sat down beside her. When everyone was talking about the war or the wedding, he asked her quietly what the doctor said about Mary's mother. She told him, and he asked how long she was likely to live.

"The doctor said three or four months in February. It's already been three. But she's not as frail as she looks. My mammy says she's always borne more than folks thought she could."

"Yes, Mary's like that too. It's Mary I'm worried about now; this is hard on her." He looked at her. "It's hard on you too, Annie; you've got big dark hollows under your eyes. Take care of yourself and your baby; there's not anything anybody can do for Mrs. Henderson."

That certainly seemed the truth.

A week after the wedding Nate left to go to Pennsylvania for training. He wrote back that he spent his days in marching and his nights singing. "They like for us to sing pack up your troubles in your old kit bag and smile smile smile but what we sing most is soupy soupy soup without a single bean porky porky pork without a streak of lean coffee coffee coffee the weakest ever seen. We sing that three times ever day at the least." With Mr. Hoover's Wheatless Monday, Meatless Tuesday, and Porkless Thursday, the Cutterfields and Hendersons at home understood what he meant. He also wrote that there were black soldiers, but they were kept in their own divisions.

In June, Ral and Hoyt had to register for the conscription, but both would probably not be called up because of their children, at least not right away.

Dr. Abbott gave Mrs. Henderson morphine for the pain until he said that he couldn't give her any more; then he gave

84

her something else that made her so wild that if she had had any strength, they couldn't have restrained her. But her wildness was better than seeing her suffer during the times when the medicine wore off before they could give her more.

She couldn't keep food; it went straight through her. That and the constant flow of blood meant that they had to keep her diapered like a baby all the time. Annie Bee ached for her every time she saw her old bony thighs. But the smell was sickening.

Their common tasks brought her and Trubie closer. The two learned to work together, one mostly caring for Mrs. Henderson and the other mostly watching the children, but each helping the other when a crisis arose. They learned to communicate with looks to keep from disturbing their patient, and Annie Bee came to think that maybe there was something to Trubie after all.

In July Trubie had to depend on Lusetta for help while Annie Bee had her baby, a boy she named Nathan. She was glad that Ral had his son, and she loved Nathan, maybe more because she was ashamed that she had resented having him so. Ral seemed pleased that he had his son, but he paid less attention to Nathan than he had to Clara.

As soon as Annie Bee could, she helped to nurse Mrs. Henderson again. The change during the few weeks since she had seen her was shocking; it was hard to think of the skeleton on the bed as someone alive. Mrs. Henderson craved sharp tastes and especially liked some corn relish Annie Bee had put up the year before. They fed it to her until it was all gone.

Fresh from bearing Nathan herself, Annie Bee kept thinking as she looked at Mrs. Henderson about the children she had borne, six that lived and three that died. It was that that was killing her, her protesting womb. Annie Bee made Ral promise that he would not make her have more.

Mrs. Henderson still had rational periods when she talked and even laughed. Once when Annie Bee was praying while watching her, she awoke from her fitful sleep. "What are you praying, child?" she asked.

"I was praying for you to get better."

"Don't ask God that. I don't want it either."

"But we all want to live."

"No, child, this is not life. And I'm not afraid of dying. What's good in me won't die. I'll either be nothing, and that'll be rest, or I'll be part of everything. And that'll be peace. But I don't want this old body. You want to pray, you pray that it dies quick."

After that, Annie Bee did.

Before Nathan was born, Annie Bee had made him a dozen new diapers to add to those that she had hemmed for Clara. But she missed them soon after she started caring for Mrs. Henderson again. At first she thought that maybe someone had mixed them with the ones used for the invalid. But her hemming stitch was different from the one Molly Lou had used. Then she checked Jacob's diapers. Sure enough, although most of them had no hem at all but were just notched along the edge, the whitest bore her stitches.

She checked several days to be sure before she confronted Trubie. Then she went out on the porch to meet Trubie as she brought a bucket of water back from the spring. "I think you got some of my diapers mixed up with yours."

"No, I got some new ones myself while you was in childbed."

"But these have my hems in them. You didn't hem yours."

"Well, I hemmed them new ones. I reckon you think nobody can't put a hem in as good as you."

Annie Bee thought of the money Ral had lent Hoyt. "I reckon most of what you've got is owed to us. But borrowing's not as bad as stealing."

"You saying I stole your dirty brat's diapers? Well, let me tell you, I wouldn't touch nobody else's belongings."

The lies on top of the thefts made Annie Bee shake. "Oh, no? What about when you and Hoyt moved out of our house and you took my best sheets to pay us for keeping you the better part of a year?"

Even in her rage Annie Bee heard the rasping cry from the sickbed. Both young women turned from each other and ran across the porch into the house. Mrs. Henderson was sitting up in bed; she raised her arms above her head, tried to call out again, and then collapsed. Her staring eyes told them she was dead before Annie Bee felt for her pulse.

When Annie Bee started to tell Ral about how his mother had died, he turned away, saying, "I don't ever want to talk about her again." Annie Bee was hurt that he closed her out; she had loved his mother too. But she knew that was his way. His eyes always locked her out.

Leathie had to go through her mother's death without Nate; he was on a ship somewhere in the Atlantic Ocean headed toward France. They all prayed that the German submarines would not attack his ship. He had written Leathie many long letters from Pennsylvania, letters she read and reread and kept under her pillow. Annie Bee knew it might have been partly Leathie's fault they had waited so long to get married, but it wasn't because she didn't love him.

Mary and Gavin did come home for the funeral. They had a telephone, and Annie Bee's mother had called them as soon as she knew. They had bought a camera and brought several pictures, not just of themselves and their car but also of their house, the town, and some of the people they had met there.

The house seemed fine to Annie Bee; it had clapboard siding, and Mary said it was made from sawn lumber throughout; no one in town used logs. There were four rooms downstairs and an upstairs bedroom with a dormer window on the front. And it had an indoor toilet and running water. The other houses in the pictures looked much like it, although some were brick and even finer, but none of them had big trees around; trees appeared only on the hills in the background of the photographs. The people had smart clothes, but the women's skirts were too short; their ankles showed.

Gavin said that there were rumors that the War Industries Board would have a big gunpowder plant built in the town on the river, so people were coming there to buy up land from the farmers. There was plenty of carpentry for him to do.

The funeral was at home, and Mrs. Henderson was buried beside her dead children in the cedar glade, where she had shown Annie Bee. Ral's face was set, and Annie Bee noticed how much his expressions were like his father's. She wanted to comfort him and to have him comfort her, but his clipped words and closed expression kept her from reaching to hold on to him.

She wondered if her quarrel with Trubie had upset Mrs. Henderson and led directly to her death, but she reminded herself that Mrs. Henderson had wanted to die. Nevertheless, she felt guilt as well as loss as she watched Ral, Hoyt, Clem, and Gavin shovel dirt onto the coffin. She and Trubie had not spoken to each other except for public greetings since their quarrel. She avoided looking at her whenever she could.

Haskell Gwaltney came to the funeral, and after the burial, Annie Bee saw him say something to Molly Lou. She acted as though he were a hole in the air. Her face looked shriveled up like a dried apple.

IV. Leaving

Molly Lou and Leathie now had full responsibility for caring for Mr. Henderson and Lusetta. Trubie took care of Hoyt and Jacob, but was pregnant again and used that as an excuse to do little. In some ways it was easier on the household than while Mrs. Henderson had required nursing, but even as ill as she had been, she had bound the family together. Since her death, Mr. Henderson had become childish and querulous, often asking where Julie was.

Leathie spent as much time as she could with Annie Bee and Ral, and she played with Clara and Nathan and talked about having her own children. She made plans for her own home as soon as Nate came home. She talked as though he would soon be there, although they all knew that it might be months or years. Or never. Every visitor coming up the wagon road brought anxiety until identified, and the black-bordered casualty list in every week's paper was scanned first.

From time to time Leathie had again received a few letters from Nate. The parts of his letters telling where he was had been censored, but she figured out from what he said that he must be in France. Wherever he was, he was homesick; Leathie said that he kept saying that he missed his little country girl and that she had to keep the home fires burning. He hadn't gotten her latest letters and still asked about her mother's health.

Annie Bee also felt that Mrs. Henderson's death had cut their ties to the family place, and since talking with Mary and Gavin, she had become excited about the idea of moving to town. Maybe they could have a better home there and a better life. If a war plant was built there, Ral could surely find work. Acey Jennings had lost money on his race track in the last two years and had sold several horses; he had not hired Ral for any training in the last year, so all the cash Ral and Annie Bee had gotten was their share of the slim income from the farm.

Her one regret would be leaving her own mother. She still joined her in gathering herbs or helping with a delivery as often as she could, although it was harder with two children of her own. Leathie came and stayed with the children sometimes; Annie Bee knew that she was pretending they were her own and Nate's, and she indulged Leathie like a younger sister. Even Callie Jane could occasionally be counted on to take care of Clara and Nathan; she was older now than Annie Bee had been herself when she had married, though still babied by their parents.

Annie Bee listened with care now when her mother told her about the herbs, when to use apple bark and when to use red alder for teas and what to gather in the dewy morning and what by moonlight. At night she wrote down what she had learned, preparing herself without thinking about it for the time when she wouldn't be close enough to ask her mother.

All the time she was planning how to get Ral to move and how to get their money back from Hoyt. For she knew they would need money. They couldn't charge things as they did at Nolan's, to pay for when the crops came in. And they would have to have cash to travel themselves and to move their belongings. Mary and Gavin had moved on the steamboat that stopped at Ridgefield every evening. Annie Bee began sorting out the things that they could move and those that they would have to leave. The things they left would have to be replaced in Old Hickory. More expense!

When she finally mentioned the idea to Ral, it was the expense that bothered him most too. She had thought he would not want to leave home, but he was restless, perhaps because of his mother's death. At any rate, his first objection was that they would lack even a roof over their heads.

"We could stay with Gavin and Mary. You know they wouldn't mind, and they have that big house now."

"We could stay there a few days, but that's all. I won't be beholden. A man's not a man if he lets somebody else support his own family, kin or not. So you just better forget about moving for a while."

Annie Bee smiled. She didn't have to forget; he had given her the words she needed to get their money back. Hoyt might be full of tomfoolery, but he was brought up the same way Ral was.

Soon after, she asked Trubie to visit her one day without mentioning it to Leathie. Annie Bee and Trubie had not been friendly but had not spoken of their rift in the family, so no one except Trubie could know that this was a motion toward peace. When she came, Annie Bee didn't mention diapers or sheets or even loans; she asked how Trubie liked living with Hoyt's family.

Trubie shrugged. "Well, course we'd rather have a place of our own, but there's no chance of that."

Annie Bee said, "Yes, I remember how glad I was to move here. This has been a good place; too bad you and Hoyt can't have it."

91

"Well, there's not much chance of that, is there? You and Ral ain't like to go nowhere else."

"Yeah, well, we would if we could. We talked about moving to town like Gavin and Mary. And that would be good for you and Hoyt. Because Mr. Henderson won't give this place to Hoyt nor Ral either long as both of them want it. Molly Lou'll get the homeplace, her and maybe Lusetta if she don't marry; Leathie and Nate'll get a place of their own soon as Nate comes home from the war. But if Ral and me was gone somewhere else, Mr. Henderson would probably give this place to you and Hoyt, straight out. It's worth more'n you'd be able to buy on your own. After Molly Lou died, your younguns would probably get the homeplace too. But I reckon there's no use either one of us dreaming; Ral and me can't move without some ready cash, so I guess you and Hoyt'll have to wait a while, too." Her seed planted, Annie Bee turned the talk to Trubie's expected second child.

Annie Bee was trying to figure out how to see Hoyt by himself when her chance came to her on its own; he came by one afternoon to get some tack when Ral was at Squire Gwaltney's with Acey waiting for a mare to foal. Giving Hoyt a cup of coffee, she asked how the crops were selling.

"Well, pretty good, I reckon; we got more rain than some, so we got a right good crop, and prices is up 'cause it's been a bad year." He poured some coffee into his saucer to cool and sipped appreciatively.

"That's good. Maybe out of your share you can pay your brother back some of the money you borrowed when you and Trubie got married."

Hoyt flushed. "Ral wouldn't never ask me for it."

"No, I reckon not, even if his own had to do without. But I reckon you know well as he does, a man's not a man if he lets another man support his family, brother or not."

Hoyt set his saucer down and stood up. "You're a hard

woman, Annie Bee. I'll see that Ral gets your money back, part of it now and the rest when I can."

"I just have my own to think about, Hoyt. And if we get some money and leave this place, I reckon it won't hurt you any. You talk with Trubie about it."

Hoyt left without finishing his coffee, much less waiting to see Ral.

A few days later, Ral came in with almost half the sum he had lent his brother. "See?" he told his wife. "I bet you thought Hoyt wouldn't ever pay us back."

Annie Bee expressed her delight and brought up the old idea of moving. Ral, as excited as she, began to plan with her.

They loaded their clothes, Clara's and Nathan's toys, bedclothes, kitchen equipment, and a few pieces of furniture on the steamboat at Ridgefield one October evening. It was cold and gray, but Ral said it wouldn't rain. Hoyt had driven them and their household goods to the boat in a wagon; they had said good-bye to everyone else at home. Trubie had been moving in as they were moving out, so the house under the pear tree would not stand empty even one night. Gavin would meet them at Old Hickory; they would stay with the O'Neills for a few days until they could get settled.

Annie Bee made pallets of quilts and featherbeds for them next to their barrel, chests, and bushel baskets. They would be sleeping on pallets all the time after they left Gavin and Mary's until they could afford to buy a bedstead; theirs had been too heavy to bring.

But it was not the hardness of the deck that kept her awake. Long after Ral and the children were asleep, she lay looking at the blank, dark sky, listening to the boatmen's calls. She kept seeing faces, especially her mother's, with tears running down the wrinkles. She would not see her again for a long time—nor Leathie nor her father nor Callie Jane. She who had never been farther from home than twenty miles was going to a strange town, maybe to live there for the rest of her life. And she had chosen to do this herself; she had pulled Ral away from his home when he would never have thought of leaving it himself, but would have gone on for the rest of his life sleeping in the bed he was born in and tilling the land his father and his grandfather had tilled.

And he was all now that she had to depend on. Just as his muscles had to wrest their support from the earth or an untamed horse or whatever forces held the key to getting a living in this strange place, so now his love alone would have to sustain her life—would have to be her life. She closed her eyes and prayed that this new place would be a good home for them.

In the dreary light before sunrise the boat landed at Old Hickory. Annie Bee was stiff and tired; she had slept little. The children fretted, and Ral looked grim. People were milling around everywhere, loading and unloading. They all looked anxious and unfriendly to her, but she was glad she didn't have to speak to them; she felt as if she might burst into tears.

Just then someone grabbed her around the waist from behind and swung her up into the air. Terrified, she screamed, only to see Ral break into a grin and cry, "Gavin!"

Gavin set her down and smiled; she gave him a proper hug and kiss. "I never was so glad to see anybody! All this crowd!"

Ral stayed with part of their belongings while Gavin drove her and the children and a load to his house. At first she worried about things falling out of the open car. As they drove, her excitement at seeing the town revived her. There were more houses, more streets, more stores, and more people than she ever could have imagined in one place. Even this early, people were rushing everywhere, in cars or wagons, on horseback or foot. There were black people and strange foreign-looking dark people. It was like election day and a brush-arbor meeting rolled into one. And this was just an ordinary workday!

Mary met them at her door and welcomed them in. She gave Annie Bee the choice of the second bedroom downstairs or the larger upstairs; Annie Bee chose the downstairs partly because she was too weary to carry everything upstairs and partly because she was afraid Clara would fall on the steps. Clara soon showed her mother that this fear was groundless; she climbed up the steps, bumped down them on her bottom, and then climbed up again to repeat the delightful new game. Mary and Gavin laughed at her as Gavin and Annie Bee unloaded the car.

Her fun changed to tears when she noticed a broken post on the doll bed Gavin had made her. Annie Bee felt like crying, too, but Gavin promised to fix it.

Gavin and Mary made them welcome. Gavin's thirtieth birthday fell a few days after they arrived, and Mary kept saying how good it was to have family there to celebrate. Gavin came to the table bent over a cane and wearing spectacles; he groaned about his rheumatism and pretended he was deaf. They all laughed at him until their sides hurt.

But despite their hospitality, Annie Bee as well as Ral wanted to find a place of their own and move out. Every day Ral went looking for work, and between the times she had to nurse Nathan or help Mary, Annie Bee looked for a house to rent. But so many people were coming into town, lured by talk of the powder plant, that places were hard to find. She learned that the dark, strange people in town had come all the way from Mexico to find work there. Annie Bee wouldn't take a place near the tents they lived in. She also rejected any place that seemed to have too much traffic near it; she was afraid that Clara, used to running free over the fields, would be hurt. And Nathan had learned to crawl too; soon he would be as likely to get in harm's way as Clara.

She grew tired of tramping through the mud and smelling the sooty air; the coal smoke was not like the clean smell of wood smoke, but had the oily smell of tallow candles. Everything in the town seemed new and raw; there were no schools or even churches built yet. Annie Bee missed going to church on Sunday.

Ral had no better success finding work than she had finding a house. Employers were all waiting to see if the powder plant really would come to town. If it did, they would want help; but until they knew, they feared overextending. There were rumors that the new powder mill was to be built in Charleston, West Virginia, instead of Old Hickory.

Winter came early. The first snow fell in the middle of November, and although it melted as soon as it hit the ground, it froze Annie Bee's heart. She did not want to spend the winter imposing on Gavin and Mary; they were kind and never seemed to mind, but she felt the obligation grow every day. Each morning she put on her coat and set out down the muddy streets, often breaking the ice that was like white window glass on the puddles. The frost looked like dead snow.

Just when she was giving up hope, she found a house for them. It was an old farmhouse that the town had overtaken, and it was not as large or even as fine as their old home under the pear tree. There was no indoor plumbing, so the toilet was out back. But there was a pump outside the kitchen, and Annie Bee had carried water all her life; she didn't need the conveniences Mary's health required. The well water tasted better than Mary's city water anyhow. The house had been divided into four rooms: a kitchen, a sitting room, and two bedrooms. There was a fence around the house and separating the yard from what must have been the barnlot; it would confine Clara and Nathan. The landlord said that the tall bushes in the yard were lilacs. And rent for the house was not as great as most, although Annie Bee dreaded already the dwindling of their money; they had bought food to help with their upkeep at Gavin and Mary's, and prices in town were double and triple what Annie Bee was used to, even for food so old and stale that she would have thrown it to the pigs at home. Her good shoes had been lost or left in the moving, and she had bought no new ones because they cost so much in town.

The day after she found the old house, when with Ral's permission she was going to rent it, she noticed for the first time a sign outside a house that she had often passed before: GOODS FOR SALE. A tired-looking woman opened the door at Annie Bee's knock; she had evidently been packing one of the boxes scattered around the room. Annie Bee looked over the items for sale and found exactly what she needed, a stove. "How much for this?" she asked, almost afraid to hear.

"I won't take less'n two dollars. But them skillets and kettles go with it."

Concealing her delight lest the woman raise the price, Annie Bee paid her at once from what she had brought with her for the rent and arranged for Ral to come and get the stove later. She took the cooking utensils with her and carried them back to leave at the O'Neills', get two dollars more, and tell Mary what a bargain she had found. For the first time since moving to Old Hickory, she felt really happy.

V. Work and Idle Hands

There was little besides the new house to make her happy. War news was that the Italians were being beaten by the Austrians. Ral still had found no work but seemed to spend less time at home than when he had farmed and worked for Acey too. The house was lonely. She missed her mother especially; she wished that Mammy could have seen Nathan's first smile and the first time that he sat up by himself. Nor did she and Ral make new friends in town. If there had been churches, they would have gotten to know people. One neighbor, Prue Huffines, had brought them a pot of beans and a skilletful of cornbread the night they had moved in, but she had four or five children running around and seemed busy all the time.

Annie Bee spent much of her time with Mary still, not only because she was lonely but because Mary had a sick spell again and needed someone to nurse her while Gavin was working. Annie Bee wouldn't take any money, although Gavin and Mary both tried to pay her.

Mary's doctor, Dr. Baker, watched her help Mary and started giving her the directions for Mary's care. He called her his little nurse, and one day he suggested that she work for him. "You're good with sick people, and I need someone to check on patients who need to be seen regularly but aren't in crisis. Could you do that for me two days a week?" And he named wages that more than doubled the best her mother had ever gotten, as much as a man would be paid back home, fifty cents a day. He pulled on his white beard, which always reminded Annie Bee of her father; he was little and wiry like Pap too.

Annie Bee replied that she would have to ask her husband, but she knew that Ral couldn't very well say no; they needed some income to keep from having to spend all their savings. When she told him, she was jubilant. "You know, that's my luck. I'm always finding pennies; once I found a whole silver dollar 'way out in the middle of the woods."

Ral said, "If you find them, it's because you're always looking. But what are you going to do with Clara and Nathan while you go traipsing all over town?"

Annie Bee looked warily at him; it wasn't good that he had asked that question. "Well . . . I thought maybe those two days you could watch them. Mary would, but she's too poorly."

"You thought *I* would? That's woman's work! Reckon you'll have to find somebody else or stay home and tend them yourself." He tossed his head back and gave her a smirk that dared her to find a way.

So she did. She offered Prue Huffines half of what she would get from Dr. Baker, and Prue said that was too much, but she would keep the children for less. So every Tuesday and Friday, Annie Bee went around with Dr. Baker to learn his patients and their needs. He would pull up at her house in his big Buick touring car, one with a metal roof, and she would run out and climb up over the high running board by herself. She thought it strange that the doctor, such a neat man himself with his gold watch chain looped across his buttoned vest, kept the back seat filled with all sorts of bags and boxes stacked helter-skelter.

Many of the patients that he took her to see were like Mary, victims of some chronic ailment, asthma, diabetes, or consumption. Part of her duty was to see that they did not develop new problems without telling him and that they took the medicine he gave them. He also had her attend to the pregnant women who had no apparent problems.

"You've had two children of your own, haven't you?"

"Yes, and I've also helped my mammy; she's a midwife."

He frowned. "Well, that's all right, but I don't want you to give my patients any old granny remedies—no soot or cobwebs to stop bleeding or mumbled Scripture to cure the thrush mouth."

"Yes, sir" was all Annie Bee said, but she was insulted that Dr. Baker coupled her mother with the old superstitions; Mammy had always worked with Dr. Abbott, and he sent women to her when he knew they couldn't pay him. And it was the faith healers, not midwives, who claimed to cure by Scripture.

Annie Bee learned about another kind of patient when they visited Mrs. Taylor. She spent thirty minutes talking half the time about the pain and suffering she had to endure and half the time about how Mr. Taylor was remiss in caring for her.

He hovered in the background, stubble on his chin and no shoes over his stockings, saying "Now, Pearline," but he seldom was able to contribute more.

Dr. Baker said little, too, until he gave her an assortment of varicolored pills and specific instructions for using each one.

Back in the car, he snorted. "That old biddy! Sound as a dollar! She'll outlive us all!"

"Then why did you give her all those pills?"

He looked at her. "Sugar! Just different shapes and colors

of sugar! They're just to keep her satisfied. Maybe she'll not henpeck her husband to death if she thinks she gets enough attention. Though he doesn't deserve much help—the tightwad's always trying to weasel out of paying his bills." Then he told her of other patients who were not really sick that she would be seeing. He called them "hypochondriacs."

Annie Bee wondered how giving them sugar pills was different from the faith healers' Scriptures. But of course the faith healers didn't take any payment.

Soon she was going around without Dr. Baker, seeing patients two or three times as often as he, learning things about their lives that they would never have told him. The women especially told her about symptoms that they would have been ashamed to mention to a man. But men and women alike mentioned their worries and plans and the changes that happened to them and their families. She told Ral about them until he told her to stop: he didn't care to know about a bunch of people he had never met.

Dr. Baker asked her to work more, and she began working every Thursday too. He would have had her work for him every day, but she needed some time at home to cook, clean, and do the laundry; otherwise, she was afraid Ral would make her stop nursing, money or no money. He threatened to when she raised the hems on her skirts. He said it wasn't decent; they were almost half a foot from the ground. But she told him she couldn't have her skirts dragging in the mud all the time, and her determined tone made him drop the threat, although he grumbled. He also thought up extra things to ask her to do at home, like putting more starch in his shirts or cooking for ordinary days as if they were Christmas. She knew her house wasn't as clean as his mother had always kept hers. But his mother hadn't brought home any money, either, except when she had occasionally sold some homespun.

The new job brought her closer to Prue, a tall, plain woman of about thirty whose hair and skin and eyes were all so light that she seemed to have no color at all. Her clothes and children and house were always scrubbed until they seemed to fade into nothingness too except for the smell of soap. Annie Bee came home at noon to nurse Nathan, and if Ral was not at home, she sometimes ate with Prue, whose food was as tasty as her cleaning was thorough. Walter, Prue's husband, worked over the river in Nashville and didn't come home for dinner. Prue was a good soul who reminded Annie Bee of the folks she had grown up with in Stone's Creek.

One day Annie Bee was puzzled to hear Prue refer to her three oldest children as "McCartle's younguns," and she asked, "Was—were you a widow-woman?"

Prue looked straight at her as if to gauge her reaction. "No, I warn't, though there's some calls me a grass widow. I was married to a man named Joseph McCartle before I met Walter."

Annie Bee was shocked. Good women weren't divorced; if their husbands had other women, they pretended not to know and went on with their lives. And of course they themselves would never leave their husbands for other men.

But that was just what Prue had done. She told how she had married McCartle when she was fifteen. "I was the oldest one in my family, and my paw beat us. Maw wouldn't've let him, but he beat her too. So when McCartle come and started talking to me, I took the chance to leave home. McCartle warn't no wife-beater. He was old—past forty, and hadn't never been married. Wouldn't've married me but he got tired of living alone and eating his own cooking. And he was good enough to me—better'n my paw ever was.

"But then when we had been married six or seven years, he fell and hurt his back and hired Walter to take care of things. And Walter was just a couple of years younger'n me, and always coming around helping me with the heavy work and playing with the children and bragging on my cooking, and it got so we just had to have each other. And I went and told McCartle, and he told me to get off the place and take the

103

children with me. And he went to the law and divorced me.

"And I was glad, and I been glad ever since. I know some folks say I'll spend eternity in Hell for it, but I reckon living here with Walter's close as I want to come to Heaven nohow." Her face shone so that she didn't seem plain anymore.

Annie Bee didn't tell Ral about her new knowledge. She thought about looking for someone else to take care of the children, but then she decided that, grass widow or not, Prue was as good a woman as she had ever met.

There was some kind of civil war in Russia, and Russia made peace with Germany. Gavin and Ral talked when they met about that meaning the Germans had more men to fight the Allies; they thought there would be more trouble in France. Annie Bee hoped that Nate wasn't there after all or that he would not have to be in any fighting. But a letter from Leathie said that he was expecting to be in battle soon. He was excited about it.

The winter was as bitter as it had been early. Ral still had no job, and he was drinking almost every evening, either at home or somewhere else. One of the war laws had prohibited the sale of liquor, but white lightning was always available. Ral wouldn't talk with Annie Bee about the drinking or a job or anything else that mattered.

She kept busy working at home or nursing Dr. Baker's patients for pay or helping Gavin nurse Mary for nothing. She was glad to be of use to Gavin and Mary; she felt as though she was paying them back for keeping her and her family.

She came down with a cold herself at the beginning of

December and lost a whole week's work. She and Ral had to use more of their scarce reserves for the rent and food. After that she took greater precautions not to get chilled or miss meals; they couldn't afford for her to be sick. She wondered what would happen to the family if she were to have a serious illness.

Frequent light snows and lingering ice made her walking treacherous. But sometimes in the early evening when she would be coming home, she would walk down to the river and climb down a bluff to the scrubby bushes that clung to the rocks, or she would go to the edge of town and look at the tall trees on the hills where she could see them with no houses or roads or people between. It made her feel peaceful to sit and watch the gray water of the river move on and on, always changing, always the same, or to see the patterns of the bark and roots of the trees and the rocks of the hillside. The only trees in town were limber sassafras, shooting up in the new-cleared ground.

The week before Christmas, she walked to the open fields and knocked on the door of the closest house. When a woman answered, she asked if she knew whose land it was, but the woman didn't know. She asked the other neighbors, but they didn't either. So the next day she took Ral's ax and walked to the fields and cut down a little cedar for a Christmas tree, hoping no one would see her; she had never deliberately stolen anything before, except Artemesia, and she would have paid someone for the tree if she had known whom to pay.

Clara and Nathan were delighted with the tree. Nathan wanted to pull off the gray-green, rough-pointed seeds; Annie Bee distracted him with supper and put him to bed. Then Clara helped string popcorn to wrap around the tree and insisted that she had to wait up till Daddy came home to see it. Annie Bee sat with Clara on her lap and inhaled the familiar, clean smell of the cedar.

They waited, Annie Bee making up songs to lighten the time. She told Clara about the first Christmas tree she had ever seen. Someone had heard about Christmas trees and wanted one for the church in Stone's Creek, but no one knew to stand it up in a bucket. So they had hung it upside down from the rafters.

Clara said that if they hung their tree upside down, Daddy would laugh at it.

But Ral did not come home until Clara had fallen asleep. And when he did, he was drunk and vomited all over the floor.

Annie Bee carried Clara to her bed, hoping not to awaken her. When she came back into the front room, Ral was lying on the floor moaning. She swelled with rage above him. "Fine mess you make for me to have to clean up."

He struggled to his feet and slapped her. "About time you cleaned up something around here 'stead of gallivanting all over town acting smart." He swayed and would have fallen, but she caught him and led him to their bed. She cried in frustration while she cleaned up the floor. Then the stench and the humiliation of his remembered slap dried her tears.

VI. Another Death

January was so cold that the river froze over. No one could ever remember that happening before. People came to look at it; the more daring slid out onto it, and some improvised skates. Annie Bee took Clara down to see it, and the child talked for days afterward about the hard river.

Annie Bee and her mother had written each other every week, but no letter came from Christmas till the middle of the month, and then it was from Callie Jane; Mrs. Cutterfield had been ill and didn't feel like writing herself. She had had bad headaches, and her eyes had bothered her; she was afraid of going blind. Annie Bee thought of the frozen river and felt locked in town as if in a jail; she would have taken the first boat home if she could have.

Mary, too, was in bed again. Her color was a sick yellow; the doctor said that her kidneys were failing. Gavin had built a shop on the side of his garage so that he could watch her while making cabinets and furniture, but sometimes he had to work on some house that was being built. Then Annie Bee sat with her.

One day when Mary seemed especially ill, Annie Bee came back to sit up part of the night so that Gavin could get some sleep. He had moved into the other downstairs bedroom, but that night he stayed with Mary awhile even after Annie Bee came; she thought that he seemed to keep Mary alive by the strength of his will. But of course for years he had kept her alive simply by sparing her and by nursing her as tenderly as any woman could.

He looked at Annie Bee just then and smiled, and she felt as though his smile pulled something in her chest. Frightened, she looked down. It would be terrible to be in love with Gavin. She buried the cold thought as deep inside her as she could.

One of Dr. Baker's hypochondriac patients that Annie Bee saw every week was Mrs. Lammington. She complained of her heart and sat all day being waited on by her three daughters, Victoria, Roberta, and Alicia. She kept a fire in her bedroom so hot that Annie Bee felt sweat drip off her whenever she called there. The room had a sickening smell of perfume and flesh. Annie Bee had never seen Mrs. Lammington out of her bed or a lounge chair.

Dr. Baker said that Mrs. Lammington's husband, who was diabetic, was sicker than she. Because the servants gossiped with Annie Bee when she came, she knew as well as Dr. Baker that most of Mr. Lammington's trouble came from his drinking. Fortunately, he had inherited enough money that he owned a grocery store and could pay someone else to run it.

Annie Bee felt sorry for the daughters. They were all old enough and pretty enough to get married, but their mother got rid of any men who came courting them.

One night when she and Ral had already gone to bed, Dr. Baker's knocking roused them, and he asked Annie Bee to go with him to care for Victoria, the oldest girl. "She has some excessive bleeding that I want watched, and her mother is not well enough to sit up with her all night. They will pay you well for nursing her—two dollars a night. But since this is a female trouble, the family won't want it talked about. I'm sure that you will be discreet about it."

Annie Bee thought that Dr. Baker sounded like a schoolboy giving a speech he had memorized for recitation day, but she agreed to take care of Victoria.

When Dr. Baker brought Annie Bee to the Lammingtons' house, he opened the door himself and led her back to the girl's bedroom. Annie Bee wondered where the maid was; she knew that the two womenservants lived in the house. Victoria had her own room, and no one was there with her either. She was asleep, but her face was pinched with pain.

Dr. Baker said, "She's had a sedative. She should sleep for at least another hour, and whenever she wakes, you should change her dressing." He showed Annie Bee the dressings that she was to use and instructed her to burn them in the fireplace when she took them off.

Annie Bee thought that it was a shame; they were good muslin cloths, and a little cold water would take out fresh blood. They could have made good diapers. But she said that she would burn them. Indeed, the doctor made her promise to burn them all. He told her to give Victoria another sedative at two o'clock, and he would be back himself by eight o'clock the next morning. Then he left.

By Victoria's lapel watch on the bedside table, it was almost ten already. Annie Bee settled down to a night of struggling against sleep. She looked at the girl, who was really almost as old as Annie Bee and was taller by two or three inches. But her face still seemed very young, rounded like a child's.

The room was beautiful, although hotter than Annie Bee was used to. There was paper printed with flowers on the wall, and all the furniture was painted white with bedcovers and cushions the colors of the flowers. There was a whole row of little figurines, china ladies in delicate-colored dresses, across the mantel. The fire had not been banked, and there was ample wood to keep it going for several days.

Victoria woke up a little after eleven. Annie Bee asked how she was, and she said, "It hurts." Tears flowed down her face with no more restraint than a ten-year-old's.

"I'll try to be easy, but I need to change your dressing," Annie Bee said.

"Go ahead. Everybody does whatever they want to with me anyhow."

Annie Bee said nothing, but changed the dressing as gently as she could. "Have you been bleeding like this for long?"

"Just since the doctor did it."

She didn't see an incision. "Did he operate on you?"

"You might call it that. I guess they didn't tell you, did they? No, I guess Mother wouldn't want them to. Well, *I'll* tell you. They took my baby." Her mouth twisted, and she looked older.

Annie Bee had heard about this before, had heard women ask her mother if she could take their babies, make them lose them, or if she could fix them so that they couldn't have any more. But she had never known that doctors actually could take a baby. Or that they would. "Did you want to keep the baby?"

"Yes, but Mother carried on so, about how her heart couldn't bear it, how the disgrace would ruin her life, that I told them to go ahead. They didn't tell me it would hurt like this." She looked angry.

"It hurts to have a baby too."

"Yes, but then I'd have the baby. And Wendell too."

"Did he—the father?—want to have the baby?"

"Oh, yes. We planned together to have it. We figured it was the only way to make them—make her let us get married. But that wasn't enough. Nothing's enough. I'll have to live here till she dies, and then I'll be so old no one will marry me."

Annie Bee thought of saying, "You could run away and get married." But she didn't.

She slept most of the next day while Prue watched her children. That night and the next she spent again watching Victoria, who slept most of the time and avoided talking about herself again when she was awake.

Annie Bee spent part of the time wondering about Wendell. How had they met, and how had he seen her enough to get her pregnant? It had not been Annie Bee's experience that sleeping together once produced a baby.

She imagined that Wendell was Mr. Lammington's store manager and that after his courtship had been rejected, he had stolen in through the French doors in her bedroom to see Victoria. She pictured him as a tall, handsome man with a dark mustache who wore Sunday clothes all the time. He would be distraught at losing Victoria and his child. For surely now her mother would have her watched. He would try to see her, and if he failed, he would never marry anyone else. And Annie Bee felt sorry for Victoria and envied her too.

The pay for the three nights was more than Annie Bee usually made in as many weeks, and Dr. Baker complimented her on keeping the family's confidence, by which he meant their secret. But she didn't like to go back to care for Mrs. Lammington after that. She did look for Victoria whenever she went to the house though.

All of Old Hickory rejoiced the next week: it was definite that a gunpowder plant would be built there as soon as the weather permitted. Ral had already talked with the men who would be in charge, and he had a promise of a job building the plant and working in it. Annie Bee told herself that everything would be all right now; a man needs a job to make him feel like a man.

Rumors began about German spies in Old Hickory. A man who was climbing the town water tower was arrested; people said that he was carrying enough poison to kill everyone who drank city water. A mob took him from his jail cell and shot him before he could be tried. There were also stories of people working on farms who were putting strychnine in the milk. All of these people were reported to hide pictures of the Kaiser on their person. People with a German name or appearance were shunned even if they had lived in the area all of their lives.

A letter from Leathie included a copy of part of Nate's latest letter to her. He had been in a battle. He said that it was nothing like what he had expected. Everyone had been frightened before it began, and when it did, the noise and confusion had been like being in the middle of a big crowd caught in a windstorm. There were bombs and artillery and mines exploding all around. Some of the cavalry horses were hit, and the stink of their guts was overpowering, worse than hog-killing, Nate said. He said that he had had nightmares about the fighting ever since.

Just as Mammy had occasionally taken care of a black woman who was having a baby, sometimes Dr. Baker sent her to see black patients. One of these was Reuben Quarles, an asthmatic about seven years old. Annie Bee checked on him late every Thursday afternoon, when his mother Leona came home from work, but Annie Bee's care really did little for him; he usually had his attacks at night, waking up gasping for breath. Fortunately, his mother had learned to nurse him through these. At Dr. Baker's suggestion, she filled her house with steam whenever he was stricken, and that seemed to help. She herself had worked out a system for him to waken her: a bell-pull ran from a cowbell fastened to the ceiling to his pillowcase, where she had pinned it.

Annie Bee had not known many black people; none had lived near her in Tarpley or Stone's Creek. But she liked Leona. If Leona had been white, Annie Bee might have even been a little afraid of her, not that Leona ever seemed to menace her. But Leona seemed always to know what she wanted to do; she moved without hurry and always spoke calmly. She was a tall, thin woman with a straight back and beautiful, long hands hardened by the housekeeping work that she did. Her eyes always looked straight at Annie Bee too, but it was in waiting, not anger. She listened well when Annie Bee relayed Dr. Baker's instructions, and she watched Reuben carefully for the things Dr. Baker asked her to notice.

Annie Bee never saw her husband and didn't know whether he was dead. She wasn't even sure that Leona had a husband. Reuben had two older sisters, Flora, who was thirteen, and Mabel, who was eleven; he was the only son. His sisters cared for him while Leona was at work.

One day when Annie Bee had finished examining Reuben and was giving Leona his medicine for the week, Leona said, "It's cold outside, ma'am. Would you like a cup of coffee before you go?"

Annie Bee often had coffee with some of the white patients, but no black patient had ever asked her before. She hesitated a moment, then said, "I'd like that, thank you. It's kind of you to ask."

The Quarleses lived in a one-room house, and Leona indicated a chair by their one table while she brewed the coffee and set out cream and sugar. Clean spoons stood in a tumbler in the middle of the table beside a begonia plant. Neither woman spoke, but Annie Bee tried to think of things to talk about.

When she brought the coffee, Leona said, "I'm grateful to you for coming to see Reuben, ma'am. Dr. Baker don't take much time for colored. I hope you work for him a long time; my little stick-man needs more'n I can do for him sometimes."

"Why . . . how did you happen to go to Dr. Baker?"

"There warn't nobody else that would see Reuben. I'd done took him to Old Momma Haynes, that treats most colored folks around here. All she ever done was hang a bag around his neck with feathers and rocks and asafetida in it. I couldn't see how a thing that stunk like that could help anybody breathe better, much less somebody that was already fighting for air. So I tried to find a doctor that would see him. Dr. Baker's the first I found that would."

"How many others did you ask?"

"Three or four—anybody close enough to walk a child to."

"Why wouldn't they? My mammy was a midwife, and she saw your . . . colored women when they needed her. And Dr. Abbott—maybe he saw some too." Annie Bee tried to remember whether she had ever heard of such.

"Maybe they would, Mrs. Henderson, but them other doctors here wouldn't. And Dr. Baker, he told me never to come to his office; he's come here when Reuben was took bad, but I can't take him to the doctor's office."

"Well, I'm not a doctor, but if you need help, I'll come." Annie Bee looked at the thin little boy and imagined her Nathan sick like him. "And if you need Dr. Baker, I'll make him come!" Then she shook her head at her own presumption. "You know what I mean: I'll do my best."

Leona laughed. "I know. And I 'preciate it, ma'am."

Annie Bee knew that she did. "Call me Annie Bee," she said.

The first week in February was as cold as January had been. No one went out unless he had to. So Annie Bee was surprised to hear a knock one night just before bedtime. When Ral opened the door and she saw Gavin's face, she knew that something grave had brought him out. "Mary . . . ?" she asked.

"Mary's all right. Annie, it's your mother."

"Oh, no!" She raised her hands to her mouth and burst into tears. Ral moved over to the table but stopped by his chair. Gavin led her to a chair and gently pushed her down by her shoulders. "Is she . . . ?" She raised her head and looked at him hopefully.

He shook his head. "She didn't have any pain, Annie. Callie Jane called, and I came right over. Seems she hadn't been well for a couple of weeks, but she was feeling better. Then she went too fast for them to call the doctor even."

"Oh, Ral!" Annie Bee cried. Gavin moved aside to make room for Ral, but he still just stood by the table.

After a moment he sat down again and said, "Well, I reckon you'll want to go to the funeral."

Then Gavin knelt beside her chair and put his arm around her shoulders. She leaned against him and poured out her grief, not just for her mother but for herself; she felt that she was in some great danger. *Oh, Ral,* she thought, *don't leave me to go through this alone. If I have to find out I can, I'll know I don't have to have you.*

And having thought it, she knew that it was already true. She trembled all over, shaken by a chill that seemed to come out of her very bones.

Book Three

The Birthday of My Life
1918 to 1919

I. A Funeral

The next day, Gavin drove Annie Bee and the children to Stone's Creek for the funeral. He had called her father, and the family would delay the services until they got there. Mary was too weak to go, and Ral said that he would stay with her to make sure that she was all right; they couldn't all ride in the car anyhow. So Annie Bee held Nathan on her lap, and Clara sat between her and Gavin under the lap quilt, one little knee on each side of the hand-brake lever. To the child it was a great adventure, from the ferry ride over the now-thawed river to the wonder of the car itself.

To her mother it was a trip of despair. She felt that at the same moment she had lost her mother and her husband; Ral seemed no more to her than a rank stranger. Not one word, not one touch of comfort or even sympathy had he given her. All night on the featherbeds and quilts they put on the floor to make their bed, she had lain awake and mourning alone.

She knew that Ral still grieved over the loss of his own mother, but that was not excuse enough to make her forgive him for leaving her in this bleakness alone. He had locked himself away from her when she would have comforted him; now when she needed comfort, he had not offered her a mere sign of common human feeling.

For a while she knew from his tossing that he too was awake, but then he had fallen into the peaceful breathing of sleep and had even started snoring. Then she had resented his rest itself.

Now, riding through the brown fields past the bare trees, she was too tired to think any more about him or her mother. It was cold, too, with the wind whipping at their scarves and mufflers. Gavin had a Clarke charcoal heater for their feet, but it was like a fireplace: too hot next to it and cold only inches away. The heavy wool lap robes helped. But the chill weather outside was like that inside her; she just prayed to get through this bitter time.

Gavin talked with Clara about the world that was rushing past them. For a long time there was no other traffic, for they had started at sunrise. When they began meeting other wagons, buggies, and cars, Gavin used them to teach Clara to count. Then since vehicles were not frequent, they counted the trees or hills they passed. Clara's little head was far down in the car, so Gavin picked objects that were tall enough for her to see.

After a while Nathan went to sleep, and Annie Bee moved him into the back seat and held Clara on her lap. Then the child could see all around, and she began making her mother play the game. Now and then Annie Bee would realize that for whole minutes she had forgotten the reason for their long trip.

They often had distractions caused by the travel itself. The roads were frozen ruts, narrow and rough. They had several flat tires. Each time that happened, Gavin would have to get out, jack up the car, and repair the puncture. Sometimes another motorist would stop to help; often people from a nearby house would come out and watch until the cold overpowered their curiosity. Annie Bee would walk around to keep warm and to give Clara some exercise.

She had packed them some ham and biscuits in lard buckets and milk in fruit jars, and at noon they sat in the car and ate it eagerly; no one had been very hungry when they had eaten breakfast. In the afternoon Clara napped lying half on the seat, half on Annie Bee's lap.

Gavin began talking about the deaths of his own parents, which had happened not long after he had married Mary. "Pa died in March, and then Ma died in June. Seemed like she just couldn't go on without Pa to fuss and laugh with. But they had both had long lives, full of children and friends. Your ma's had that, too, Annie; not many people in the county's done as much for others as she has, and I don't know many as has enjoyed living more."

Annie Bee agreed and began telling Gavin about going with her mother to deliver and tend babies. She tried to explain how she felt about the women she helped and about Dr. Baker's patients that she visited.

"Yes, it's like with Mary. Even if I didn't love her, I'd be glad that I could help someone like her that needed me. I met a fellow in Old Hickory, name of Phillips, that had gone over to France back in 'fourteen when the war first started to nurse the wounded. He left 'cause he got wounded himself, but he wanted to go back. Said it made him feel like God when he could help somebody. Reckon that's some of what we mean too."

"I don't suppose Nate will hear for a while about . . . Mammy."

"No, though they telegraph news like that. But I guess from what Phillips says that it's often hard to get news to boys at the front. Leathie may know where he is now."

"No, the censors cut out anything that shows where they are so the Germans can't tell if the letters fall into their hands."

"Well, they'll get the news to him all right."

Thinking of Leathie reminded Annie Bee that she would at least be seeing again some of those faces she had left in

October. But never Mammy again alive; never again. And poor Pap; what would he ever do without Mammy? Of course, Callie Jane would take care of the house till she got married. And after, if her husband wanted the farm; Nate never had, and Cleavus, their older brother, had married Gavin's sister Sally and moved off long ago. Maybe Annie Bee herself could have got it if she and Ral hadn't gone off to Old Hickory to better themselves; there was a trick of fate for you. But she really didn't want to make pickles in Mammy's crocks and sit in Mammy's rocking chair on the porch and look out toward the Conyer place every evening.

The trouble was she couldn't think of anything she did want except for everything but the children to be different. She looked at the cedar trees on the passing hills; they were like dead black holes in the dreary landscape, and she wanted to crawl into them.

Seeing Callie Jane, Annie Bee realized that she was a woman grown: eighteen to her own twenty-one. Two years older than Annie Bee had been when she married. Pap was fifty-eight, and Mammy would have been fifty-four in May. Even Clara was already almost three. The years were going, and all the wonderful things that growing up meant—where were they?

Callie Jane told them about Mammy's illness. As Annie Bee knew, she had not felt well since before Christmas. But she had seemed better to Pap and Callie Jane the last few days; she had insisted on doing housework again. The night she died, they had been in the kitchen cooking supper. Mammy had been mixing cornbread, and she had called Callie Jane over. "You'll have to finish this," she said. Then she had gone to her chair in front of the fireplace, sat down, and told Pap, "I done all I could. It'll have to be enough." And she was gone.

Gavin held Annie Bee again while her sorrow burst out.

She realized that she was closer to Callie Jane than she had known when she saw her brother Cleavus and sisters Wilda and Idell; they almost seemed like another family Mammy and Pa had had before Nate and her and Callie Jane. Sally, Cleavus's wife, and Duncan and Joe Edward, Wilda and Idell's husbands, had of course come, and all the nieces and nephews that Annie Bee hadn't seen for years, some almost grown themselves, some that she had never seen. In addition to them, the house seemed full of strangers at first. She felt as if she had come home and found almost no one that she knew. Many she really didn't know: babies Mammy had delivered now grown up to have children of their own, people from Tarpley who had ridden or walked over to pay their respects. But gradually Annie Bee recognized others: neighbors, cousins, women Mammy and she had helped in childbirth. It seemed strange to her that though she had not thought of them for months, even years, their lives had gone on, hidden from her like water moving under the ice.

But her life was hidden too, she realized, not just from those she hadn't seen but from those closest to her, from her sister and Gavin, who were standing beside her. She bent her head and lowered her lids over her eyes.

She and Gavin and Leathie sat up with the corpse the first half of the night, talking with Cleavus and Sally, Idell and Joe Edward, and some of the Conyers. At midnight they were relieved by those who had been sleeping, Wilda and Duncan, Callie Jane, Molly Lou, and some of the Spiveys and Simmses. Orville Spivey's boy Warren had turned out to be really good-looking; Annie Bee thought that he seemed smitten with Callie Jane, who paid him no attention.

123

Annie Bee left to spend the rest of the night with Leathie as she had so often when they were girls. But now the bed they slept in was Leathie and Nate's, the one Annie Bee and Ral had used when they first married. Lusetta and Molly Lou had taken Clara and Nathan to the Hendersons' earlier, and the children were sleeping on a pallet on the floor by the bed. Gavin was staying with Cleavus and Sally.

Leathie hadn't heard from Nate since just before Christmas. "I don't even know whether he got my Christmas package. I sent him socks and a scarf I knitted and a box of boughten candy, but I haven't heard a word, and it's been almost two months." She wrinkled her forehead. "Now I don't know if he's hurt or lost or . . . worse. I don't know if he just don't want to write; he's not wrote much lately nohow." She stopped, but her look showed her desperation.

Annie Bee tried to reassure her, but she thought for some reason of Tad, Nate's pet rabbit. They had found it and its littermates in a hayfield after mowing, and being eight and five, had adopted them all whether they were orphaned or not. The kits' eyes were open, so they had a better chance of living than most. But all except three died right away. She couldn't remember what happened to the third one; hers had been named Luella and had made a meal early for their cat Minnie, much to her grief.

But Tad had lived to be almost grown, and Nate had made much of him; he said he would train him to do tricks and make lots of money. So when Pap stepped on Tad and crushed him one day when he had gotten out of his box, Annie Bee had cried just thinking about how unhappy Nate would be.

But when she told Nate, he had shrugged his shoulders. "Aw, that's all right. I'm tired of that old rabbit anyhow—it just made work cleaning up."

The next morning Annie Bee and Leathie and the children walked through an inch of new snow over to the old Henderson place to see Hoyt and Trubie's newest son, Jared. Annie Bee wished that she hadn't come and seen the house; it was dirty, and trash littered the yard already. What hurt her the most, though, was the pear tree: an ice storm had broken its limbs, and it stood like a jagged wound against the winter sky.

There were too many people to have the funeral at home, so they loaded the coffin onto a wagon and hauled it to the church, the bell tolling till they arrived. Annie Bee had looked at the body in the coffin, but the remote face there bore little resemblance to the woman she had known. She kept thinking that it would be better if they had put Mammy's starched white midwife's apron on her; she always wore one because she said she never knew when she would have to go catch some baby.

Callie Jane had given Annie Bee the ferrotype Mammy had had made when she was a newly married woman. It didn't look like her, either, although she had tried to look old then. The greenish cast of the picture was like water washing over her face.

Acey Jennings spoke to Annie Bee at the burial and sent a message to Ral that he hoped to start a new race track. His son Porter had bought a place at Cedar Springs, north and west of Nashville, and he wanted Ral to go to see him. He gave directions and the address to Annie Bee and got her address in Old Hickory.

The family all ate an early dinner from the food the neighbors had brought, and she and Gavin made their good-byes. She felt both pain at this new parting and relief that she would leave them to face people who did not know about her loss and would not remind her of it. She was glad that Pap had Callie Jane, who had turned out to be a sober, responsible girl in spite of all. She had already burned Mammy's feather tick and started scrubbing her chair and everything that she had touched while she was sick. But the house that Annie Bee left was empty of most of what had made it home.

The travelers seemed to have more flat tires on the way back than they had going. The snow was not enough to impede them: the horses pulling the buggies they passed were not even roughshod. But the snow prevented her from letting Clara run around in her thin shoes while Gavin repaired the tires. Annie Bee didn't know whether she was colder when they stopped and stood by the road, stamping their feet to keep them warm, or when they were riding with the wind whistling around them.

Once a farmer, Ikie Sykes, came from a nearby house to help them when they had a flat. He was a young, sandy-haired fellow, and his big-knuckled hands were deft in holding the patch while Gavin sealed it on. All the while they worked, he kept up a cheerful commentary about cars and their amazing speeds and his desire to get one, and when they were through, he asked them all in for a cup of coffee. Chilled to the bone, they accepted and received gingerbread as well. While Annie Bee and the children talked to his pretty little wife, Gavin gave him a driving lesson.

They had thanked the couple and Gavin was helping Annie Bee to climb up onto the running board when Ikie said, "Nice family you got there."

"Yes," Gavin said, and he grinned at Annie Bee to share the joke. "Thank you." She tried to smile but then looked down. She could feel the erratic beating of her heart.

Nightfall came long before they got home. The car's headlights on the road shone only a little more brightly than the full moon lighting the snowy fields and hills. It was bright enough that Annie Bee could distinguish the blue of Clara's coat from the brown of Nathan's blanket as they lay sleeping. She looked at the moonlit snow until it seemed to flow into her, merciless, filling all the dark places in her soul and making her see them. She felt helpless in the white light.

II. Patients

Annie Bee was frozen against Ral. She cooked for him, talked with him, slept with him as before, but she closed him out of her heart. He gave no sign of noticing. Each morning she awoke with a sick, empty feeling. She would get up in the cold and build up the fire, but she still felt as if she carried a lump of ice inside. It was like frostbite: she felt numb, but little things touched her and seared her like fire. The house seemed strange, and she was glad to get away from it on the days that she nursed, glad to think about other people's lives instead of her own.

She and Ral did get a letter from Leathie telling them that she had heard from Nate. The Germans—Fritzes, he called them—had been pressing hard, and he had been in a gassing and was sent to the field hospital briefly, although he had not gotten hurt enough to be disabled. He said that it was like smothering: he had had to fight for breath, and his eyes had watered and burned. Pain went through his whole body, and he saw men who bled out of their nose and ears. He didn't say whether any died. He said that since then, he ran to get away whenever he heard a shell land if it didn't explode right away. Annie Bee knew that Leathie was relieved to hear from him, although she would worry more about his safety.

Annie Bee thought again of the distances between her and Ral, who shared her table and bed.

One afternoon when she had gone to watch Mary for a while, she found Mary and Gavin in the middle of an argument. She couldn't tell what it had begun about; it had reached the point where Mary was saying, "You always treat me like a child," and Gavin responded, "You never tell me what you want."

He had left the room then, closing the door, and Mary apologized for the disagreeable atmosphere.

Annie Bee said, "That's all right. Everybody quarrels, I reckon."

"He never asks me what I want. He just goes ahead and does whatever he thinks I want."

Annie Bee thought that wasn't such a bad crime; at least he was trying to please her. She wasn't sure Ral ever wondered what she wanted when he was deciding something.

Then she thought too how this showed that the O'Neills had their own differences. Their marriage wasn't so perfect after all. Maybe they didn't even love each other. Maybe Gavin didn't even love Mary.

The Lammingtons gave her mind other occupation for a while. Mrs. Lammington had a "spell with her heart," Dr. Baker told Annie Bee, raising his eyebrows and extending his lower lip to indicate his doubt about its physical basis. She wanted Annie Bee to sit up to watch her at night. Annie Bee wondered why Victoria, Roberta, and Alicia couldn't perform that daughterly duty, but she accepted the job as a way to be out of the house as well as to earn more money than usual.

She was to sit up with Mrs. Lammington every night from eight until seven the next morning, when the maid, Deborah, would take over her duties. Deborah let her in the first night and said that she would see her in the morning.

It was dull work. Annie Bee felt that she wasn't earning her wages if she went to sleep, but there was nothing she could do to keep herself awake. Her patient was propped up on four or five fat pillows snoring like a healthy woman. Annie Bee inventoried the room, evidently Mrs. Lammington's alone; there was no evidence of Mr. Lammington ever staying there. On a table with a fringed cover by the bed was what Annie Bee had come to recognize as the shrine of the hypochondriac: bottles holding syrups and elixirs and numbers of little white envelopes holding pills and powders. Spoons, glasses, a water pitcher, and a stack of handkerchiefs were also there.

The room was larger than Victoria's but like hers had its own fireplace, French doors, and printed paper on the walls. Annie Bee counted all the red nosegays on the wallpaper but couldn't remember how many there were, so she counted them again. Then she tried to figure how many there would be behind the massive bedstead, dresser, chifforobe, and chest of drawers. Then she counted all the little china figurines around the room. Mrs. Lammington seemed partial to representations of dogs. There was also a painting of a long-eared, long-haired red hunting dog that Annie Bee thought Nate would call a setter. She looked in vain for any books in the room and resolved to bring her Bible the next night. There was no sewing or fancywork, although a column of fancy pincushions hung beside a mirror framed in gilded, carved wood.

Mrs. Lammington awoke once and asked for water, then told Annie Bee to get her bedpan. It was no easy task to fit the bedpan under her pillowlike thighs and buttocks, and she complained at being exposed to the "cold night air," although Annie Bee had kept the fire going, as Deborah had instructed her, and the room seemed close. Mrs. Lammington directed Annie Bee to the bathroom, and by the time Annie Bee returned with the emptied bedpan, her patient was asleep again.

The next morning Mrs. Lammington awoke at seven and asked for her bedpan, then her breakfast, so Annie Bee took her order and was prepared to cook the meal. But she found Willadene, the housekeeper, already in the kitchen with the eggs in a skillet and the rest of breakfast on a plate.

"You've already got everything ready," Annie Bee said.

"Yes'm. A body don't work in this house twenty year without knowing to get Miss Mamie's breakfast 'fore she misses it. She don't get her breakfast on time, there be a ruckus sure 'nuff."

The smell of the sausage was making Annie Bee hungry herself. "Will the rest of the family eat soon too?"

"No, ma'am, nobody else in this house gets up before ten 'cept Miss Roberta, and she won't be getting up that early these days, I reckon." Willadene laughed as though she had told a joke.

"Why? Is she sick too?"

"Lordy, child, ain't they told you nothing? No, I reckon they wouldn't. Miss Roberta done run off with that no-count Reddenberry boy lives down the street. Reckon she seen how it went with Miss Victoria—I mind you took care of her when she had her trouble, so I reckon you know 'bout that, 'less'n nobody told you then neither—and she warn't going to let her mammy rule *her* that way. Miss Roberta, she always been a sly one: don't breathe a word to nobody till she done up and gone. Why, girl, that's why you here: that's why Miss Mamie pitch such a fit they send for the doctor and make him give her something to make her sleep all the time. Mr. Horace, he don't need such long as Wendell Phelps'll bring him his bootleg whiskey."

The eggs had put been on the plate and the plate on the tray with coffee and a bunch of violets before this speech was finished, so Annie Bee thanked Willadene and took the tray to her charge. She had quite enough to occupy her thoughts for a while.

That night when Deborah let her in, the maid grinned conspiratorially. "Willadene says she told you all about Miss Roberta. What you reckon going to happen when she come back?"

Annie Bee shook her head but said nothing. She was glad, for just then Victoria came through the open sitting-room door. "Deborah, you need to show Mrs. Henderson to my mother's room. And you aren't paid to gossip about the family in this house." She gave Annie Bee a tight-mouthed look too.

Annie Bee was shocked at the change in Victoria. Her round face had been childlike before; now it was pudgy. She must have gained twenty pounds in the few months since Annie Bee had tended her.

Two nights later Deborah hurried her into the hallway leading to Mrs. Lammington's room and, having looked around at the closed doors there, whispered, "Miss Roberta's done come back. And she brought Mr. Emory with her, and Miss Mamie went clean out of her head and said she had to have the marriage an— an— something that means it's like it never was, and Miss Roberta said it was already going to be in the papers, 'cause she and Mr. Emory done had their picture made and sent them to the papers, and it's going to say, 'Miss Lammington Weds Mr. Reddenberry,' and there ain't nothing Miss Mamie can do about it." Deborah could not have seemed more pleased if she had bested Mrs. Lammington herself.

"How is Mrs. Lammington?"

"Well, the doctor was here and give her more stuff to make her sleep. And if she wakes up, you're supposed to give her this."

Annie Bee thought of the morphine Dr. Abbott had given her for Ral's mother. Was that what kept Mrs. Lammington quiet all the time?

Often Annie Bee escaped from home to sit with Mary, who was still bedfast most of the time. There seemed little they could do for her; the doctor said that she was only hanging on by will. Ral, Gavin's friends, and even Prue and Walter took turns sitting with her too. They did not try to stay up with her all night, for her illness seemed to weaken her gradually rather than to thrust her into sudden crises.

As Annie Bee sat watching Mary rest, she convinced herself that Gavin did not love this ailing wife as a woman, but as a patient, someone who needed his care and therefore his love. She thought back to their trip to Stone's Creek for her mother's funeral; he had said something like that then about caring for Mary that way, she remembered. Mary could give him nothing—no children, no help, not even bed dues—nothing except an object for his concern and dedication. He must know that, whether he admitted it to himself or not.

But *she* could give him those things. Already she knew that he was close to Clara and Nathan. As she had watched him play with them, she had imagined that they were his or that she would give him the children that Mary never could. How he would love his own children! Surely then he would know the paleness of this love that he had for Mary.

She turned away from the bed as if she feared that the sleeping Mary could read her mind.

Mary never spoke to Gavin or Ral of dying, but to Annie Bee she gave instructions for her funeral and burial and the disposition of her belongings. She wanted to be buried at Stone's Creek in the Henderson cedar glade if they could take the body back there. She had certain brooches, books, and handkerchiefs that she wanted to be given to certain brothers and sisters. She handed Annie Bee a green brooch in a silver setting. "Gavin give it to me while we was courting," she said. She tried to get Annie Bee to take it at once, but Annie Bee wouldn't, although it reminded her of Gavin's green eyes.

Mary asked that Molly Lou be given all her clothes; no one else in the family was tall enough to wear them. She added, "If I could, I'd give Gavin to her too; he needs someone to be a real wife to him."

Annie Bee gripped tightly the pencil she had been using to write down Mary's instructions. At least she hadn't needed to worry about Mary knowing her thoughts! And in the long run, it didn't matter what she wanted or Mary wanted; Gavin would make his own choices. Not that that was a comfort to her, or would be to Mary. He would never think of choosing her, for sure: his wife's brother's wife.

There was another question that Mary's bequest raised. "But Molly Lou's married to that man from Ridgefield, Mr. Elliott, isn't she?"

"No, he divorced her when she wouldn't come back to him. But Molly Lou never told Ma; you know how Ma would've been shamed to think of anybody in the family being divorced. Haskell Gwaltney's the only one in Stone's Creek besides me that knows it; he found out through some lawyer at Ridgefield that he knows. Molly Lou said he sent word to her once to see if she'd let him court her again, but she told him she was still married to Mr. Elliott, law or no law."

"Was she just trying to get rid of Squire Gwaltney?"

"Well, I'm closer to Molly Lou than anybody else, I reckon, and I never did know whether she wanted Haskell or not. Don't know if she knows herself. But I reckon she wouldn't ever marry no one, Haskell or Gavin or whoever, 'less Mr. Elliott died. Else it wouldn't be nothing but adultery."

The word sank into Annie Bee's mind like a rock into the creek.

Leathie wrote that Nate's latest letter told of more fighting. Two of his buddies from camp had died of sickness, and another had been shot when they were charging the Germans across an open field; he had fallen on top of Nate, who couldn't move without risking their both being shot again. So his buddy had bled on top of him until he died.

The fighting had been fierce all spring. The newspapers reported that the Germans had driven the Allies back almost to Paris, and it was feared that the city was doomed.

Construction of the powder plant finally began in May, and Ral had all the work he could do, dawn till dusk. He got more pay for one day's work than he would have gotten for a week's in Stone's Creek. Annie Bee started adding to their savings again instead of taking out all the time. They bought a few things that they had needed but done without; the only clothes that they had bought had been for the growing children. Annie Bee bought material and had Prue make her a dress, the first she had had new since right after Clara was born. She felt dressed up in it when it was done; no one in town wore homespun. Ral bought a new straw hat and trousers to replace his farmer's overalls. They bought a proper bedstead, one made of iron, and even a real mattress, not just straw ticks.

Ral suggested that Annie Bee could quit her job now that he had one, but she pointed out that they would just get a place of their own sooner if she worked too. He complained that the children and the housework needed more attention. He seemed particularly offended that she had not burned out her skillets since they had moved. But she ignored his complaints. The children loved Momma Prue, as they called her, and enjoyed playing with her children, and though Annie Bee's house wasn't as clean as she would like sometimes, that seemed a small price for the security her job gave them.

After all, he had been out of work a long time; who knew whether this new job would last?

Gavin was working day and night, too, carpentering on new houses for the people moving to Old Hickory so much that he didn't have time to make furniture. Annie Bee had not seen him for several days when he came one night while the Hendersons were having supper. His unexpected coming reminded her of the night that he had told her of her mother's death. And again he did have bad news: Nate had been wounded. Leathie had gotten a telegram that he had been hit in the leg by shrapnel and was in a hospital somewhere in France. She didn't know how bad his wound was. She had telephoned Mary from the Cutterfields' to get word to Annie Bee.

"How did Pap take it?" Annie Bee asked.

"Pretty well, I reckon. But Leathie said Callie Jane said he's not eating right and don't take much interest in things. She had to fuss at him to get him to put out a garden this spring."

They went on to talk of Mary and the powder plant and the new people flooding into town every day, but Annie Bee kept thinking about Nate, who had never been still a minute of his life, lying day after day in a hospital. And heaven knows what filth he had to put up with; everybody knew how dirty those Frenchmen were. She wished that she could talk to Leathie.

The secretary at Dr. Baker's sent Annie Bee to a new address one morning. She said that a neighbor had come by and asked the doctor to see to a Mrs. Mayhew, so it might be a charity case.

The house supported her speculations. Barely more than a shack, it looked more like an old outbuilding than a human dwelling. The small windows on each side of the door were two holes cut in the wall with unbleached domestic tacked up to keep out the weather.

The child who opened the door to Annie Bee's knock was not much older than Clara, and Annie Bee couldn't tell whether it was a boy or a girl. Its hair was uncut and uncombed, and its dress and skin were gray with dirt. "Are you here to help my momma?" it asked. Another younger child was sitting by the potbellied stove in the middle of the room, drooling over its fist, and a baby tethered to a table leg was trying to crawl toward the stove. The whole room smelled of dirty diapers.

"Yes. Where is she?"

The child put its finger in its mouth, then pointed toward a heap of rags on some piece of furniture behind the stove. "Over there."

The light inside was dim, and it took Annie Bee a moment to find the woman's face. Her eyes were closed and her skin red. Annie Bee felt her forehead: she certainly had fever, and not a low one. "Mrs. Mayhew! Can you hear me?"

The woman stirred and opened her eyes, but didn't seem to focus on Annie Bee. "Water. Please, give me some water."

After looking vainly for a clean glass, Annie Bee took the least dirty from the dishes on the table and filled it from the water bucket by the stove. She held the woman up enough to drink; she seemed almost too weak to swallow.

When she was through, she said, "Go get my husband. I got rid of the baby, but I'm going to die."

"Where is he?"

"Down at Cole's. Drinking."

Annie Bee could not imagine any benefit from adding a drunken husband to the situation. "Is there anybody else who can help?"

"Maybe Mrs. White." That was the neighbor who had sent for Dr. Baker; she had told the secretary that she worked in someone's home all day. "You got something to ease me?"

Dr. Baker let Annie Bee give people aspirin, so she put two far back on Mrs. Mayhew's tongue and tipped the glass of water up for her to drink. She almost choked on the aspirin, so Annie Bee made her drink more water.

Annie Bee didn't know what to do first. If what the woman said was true and she had tried to do away with a baby, she needed Dr. Baker right away. But Annie Bee hated to leave the other three children in such conditions.

"Please! Go get my husband."

"I will," Annie Bee replied. But she resolved to get anyone else she could first—any woman.

Telling the oldest child to stay with its mother and to keep the others there, she went into the street and knocked on the next door. She was relieved when a clean-looking woman answered. "Excuse me, but your neighbor's in a bad way. Would you please watch her and her children till I can get back with a doctor?"

"I got younguns of my own I can't leave. And how do I know you'll come back nohow?" The woman closed her door.

There was no one home at the next house. But at the third the woman, a Mrs. Haynes, agreed to come and herded her own two boys ahead of them. "The poor child!" she said when she saw Mrs. Mayhew. Then Annie Bee realized that Mrs. Mayhew was probably not past twenty.

After the hurried walk to Dr. Baker's, Annie Bee found that he was out. She explained the situation to the secretary and asked her to send Dr. Baker as soon as she could.

"I'll try, but he's got more *paying* patients than he can take care of," she replied.

Back at the Mayhews, she found that Mrs. Haynes was doing more than just watching the sick woman. She had gotten wood somewhere—Annie Bee had noticed before that there was none in the house or near the stoop—and had built a fire and was heating water. She helped Annie Bee examine Mrs. Mayhew, who was again unconscious. Together they removed the bloody rags covering the broken sofa that served as a bed. Mrs. Haynes went home and brought back clean sheets, towels, a gown, and several cuptowels. By then the water was hot, so Annie Bee washed the girl as well as she could while Mrs. Haynes changed the bed. The two women dressed the girl and settled her on the clean bed. She groaned all the time.

Then they cleaned up the children, washing them all over, hair and all. They were two little boys and a baby girl. Mrs. Haynes used the cuptowels for diapers for the younger two and brought an outgrown outfit of her own boy's for the oldest.

And Dr. Baker had still not come. Annie Bee checked the mother again.

"How is she?" Mrs. Haynes asked.

"Not good. She seems to be sinking."

"Lord help us! And what'll happen to these little ones?"

"She's got a husband. Wanted me to fetch him, but she said he'd be drinking, so I wasn't in a hurry."

"Probably with that bunch down at Cole's on the corner. Ever since so many new people come to town, this neighborhood ain't fitting to live in."

"Yes, that's where she said he'd be. Do you think I should get him?"

"Reckon if she's going, you ought. I'll watch the young-uns."

Annie Bee had seen the store on the corner with the sign saying COLES. She told herself it would be like Nolan's or the store in Old Hickory where she had shopped since Mary had introduced her to it, but she still dreaded going in.

It looked all right, like most stores she had been in, except that the men in the back corner near the unlit stove were passing a bottle around without even trying to hide it and were playing with poker cards instead of checkers. They all stared at her when she came in. "Is there a Mr. Mayhew here?"

One of them leered at her. "Lordy, Rod, what you been up to now to have a good-looking woman like that come after you?"

A young man already wobbly-eyed waved his cards at her. "I'm Rod Mayhew, sugar. What you got for me?"

"I've got a message that your wife's bad off and asking for you."

"Aw, she's always wanting something. Don't want me to have no fun. You tell her . . . you tell her I'll come when I'm good and ready. And I'm good now, but I ain't ready."

The men laughed at his wit. Annie Bee left in disgust and relief that he hadn't come with her.

Mrs. Haynes was not surprised at her report. "I'll go get us some dinner, Mrs. Henderson, and maybe the doctor'll come."

Annie Bee didn't tell her, but she didn't have much faith that he could do anything if he did. Mrs. Mayhew had stopped groaning, and her skin was ashen now instead of flushed. Annie Bee checked her weakening pulse every few minutes. She was still bleeding in floods.

They ate the food Mrs. Haynes brought. The two older Mayhew children ate as though for the first time in a week; the baby cried weakly, and the women decided she had not yet been weaned. They spent some time teaching her to drink from a teacup.

Mrs. Haynes said, "It just proves some women can get with child again before they quit nursing. Reckon that's how come she's got so many so close together."

"That, and that drunken lout down at Cole's."

They spent the afternoon waiting for Dr. Baker, not talking about the woman but about what would happen to her children. Annie Bee went back to the store once to try to persuade her husband to come home, but he was lying passed out on the floor. About four in the afternoon his wife died, and Annie Bee went back to tell the storekeeper. Mrs. Haynes had taken the children home with her to keep until their father or someone took them.

Dr. Baker was at the office when she went back. She told him what had happened, and he grunted. "I probably

couldn't have helped her. What women will do to themselves!"

"You helped Victoria Lammington."

He looked at her then. "I didn't know whether you knew
about her or not. Well, this case was entirely different. Entirely. Don't suppose we'll collect anything, but I'll send
them a bill for your time. Now, these are the patients you
need to see next. Try to work in some extras to make up for
those you missed today."

A few days later, as soon as she found time, Annie Bee
checked with Mrs. Haynes. Mrs. Mayhew's mother had
come and gotten the children. The women shared their relief
that they had not had to go to an orphanage.

III. Fever

In July the gunpowder plant opened. The Nashville newspaper said that twenty thousand people had come to Old Hickory since January, many of them immigrants from Mexico. Dr. Baker had more patients than he could see, so he persuaded Annie Bee to work four days a week. Ral worked six days a week and often carried his supper as well as his dinner with him, and Prue kept the children, so Annie Bee had less to do at home.

Shortly after she began working more, there was a terrible train collision on the other side of Nashville at a place called Dutchman's Bend. Almost two hundred fifty people, many of them Mexicans coming to work at the powder plant, were killed or injured. Dr. Baker was called on to help with the injured, so for over a week she had to see all his patients in Old Hickory and send those who needed him at once to the one doctor still in town. When he had returned and seen his patients again, Dr. Baker complimented her on her judgment.

She and Prue ate lunch together every day unless she was seeing patients too far away, and she shared her worry about Nate and the families at Stone's Creek with Prue. Prue hadn't kept up with her own family; her mother was dead, and her father had disowned her when she had left McCartle.

"Don't you ever miss seeing them?"

" 'Course I do, even if Pappy did beat me. But I give them up for Walter."

"Are you ever sorry?"

She shook her head hard. "No. Oh, I ain't glad I sinned, but I wouldn't have had no kind of life with McCartle. I miss having friends more'n I miss kin. You know, you're the only woman friend I got; ever'body else is ashamed to say they know me." She looked down to hide her full eyes.

Annie Bee reached out and squeezed her hand. "I'm proud to have you for a friend."

After a pause, Prue went on. "You're the best friend I ever had, and I'm grateful for you. But I know what I done ain't right, and I just pray to the Lord ever' day that He won't take it out on my innocent children."

"Oh, He wouldn't do that. Maybe the beatings your pappy gave you when you was a youngun paid you out."

"Well, I don't know if the Lord counts like that. But I don't mind paying hereafter for what I do; I just don't want my little ones to suffer."

Annie Bee tried to reassure her. Still, one never knew. She watched Clara and Nathan as they played on the floor with the fair-haired Huffines and the dark-haired McCartles.

In the fall influenza swept the country. The newspapers at first reported a few cases, then more, and finally began listing only the deaths. Dr. Baker told Annie Bee what to tell people to do and sent her out to see people he had not even examined; there were too many for the few doctors in the town to see even if they worked day and night. Influenza victims were treated mainly with diuretics to wash the disease out of their systems. But now so many were sick that most got no medicine at all. It was all Annie Bee could do to feed soup to those who were well enough to eat and to clean the rest up as best she could. At night she heard the dead wagons rolling through the streets.

Then Mary took influenza. She had been pretty well during the summer, but had no strength to fight this new onslaught. Annie Bee had not gone near her since the epidemic because she didn't want to take it to her, but now Gavin, Annie Bee, and Ral took turns sitting with her. She was fevered all day and kept calling for water. She said that the top of her head hurt and rubbed it into the mattress until Annie Bee thought that she would rub her hair off like a baby.

Mary grew worse, delirious all the time, and Gavin would not leave her even when the others came. Once while Annie Bee was watching her and he was pacing the floor, he broke down and sobbed. Annie Bee rose and stood behind him and, holding his arm with one hand, helplessly patted his back with the other.

Finally he sat down, shaking his head back and forth. "Oh, Annie, Annie, if she dies, there's nothing left for me."

She knelt beside the chair and held his head against her shoulder and stroked his unruly hair, speaking the old lying words of comfort, her voice even, sure, until he calmed himself. And all the time she thought, *He loves her, not me. Never me.*

Later the other thought came: *Ral never loved me like that. No man ever loved me like that.* She wished for her mother; she wished that she could put her head in her mother's lap and cry and cry until there was nothing left in her mind.

She was somewhere in the dark. It had been dark for a long time, but until now, the darkness had been full of fire and noises, people talking, strange laughing. Now the dark was quiet, cool. And there was some light, but it came from behind her. She turned over.

She was at home in her own bed. Ral was sitting in a chair looking at her, the lamp beside him shaded so that its light wouldn't fall on her. He got up when he saw that she was awake. "How are you?" he asked.

"I don't know. What happened? How did I get home? I was sitting up with Mary."

"But you took sick yourself. You been out of your head for days—kept talking about Prue, and Hellfire and brimstone, and Mary taking care of Clara and Nathan."

"How is Mary?"

He didn't answer for a bit. "She—they buried her three days after you took sick."

Annie Bee remembered Mary's kind, gentle face and began to weep without sound. The tears slipped down her cheeks and seemed to drain her of the little strength she had. Ral pulled the covers over her shoulders and carried the light out with him.

When she was well enough to be up again, Annie Bee found the list of Mary's instructions for her funeral and her bequests. All given for nothing. Annie Bee knew from talking with Ral and Gavin that she had been buried at home in the cedar glade and that Molly Lou had gotten her clothes; no one else could wear them. As for the other things, Gavin had distributed them himself. She didn't know who had the green brooch; Gavin gave her a gold ring with a circle of pearls all around a cameo as a remembrance. It fit only her middle finger, but when she regained the weight she had lost, it would fit her ring finger.

144

Nate had written Leathie two or three letters from a hospital somewhere. They said that he was recovering and would be sent back to the front as soon as he could. The Allies had kept the Germans from taking Paris and were even pushing them back.

Hoyt brought Trubie, Jacob, and Jared to visit in October. Trubie was pregnant again. They stayed at Gavin's larger house but ate with Ral and Annie Bee, as Gavin did. The first night after supper, Hoyt presented to Ral the rest of the money they had borrowed; it had been a good growing year with good prices. Annie Bee thanked them and wished them success in farming the homeplace. Trubie thanked her and complimented them on the house they had. Ral said that it was just rented, but they were looking for a place of their own. Annie Bee looked at him quickly, and he nodded. Altogether, it was a most satisfactory visit.

Having Gavin visit with Hoyt and Trubie made Annie Bee think about asking him to eat with them. She felt guilt about suggesting it to Ral, but the hunger in her heart was greater.

To her surprise, Ral agreed at once. "It's just common help to a friend, much less a brother-in-law."

The next day she went to Gavin's house and, getting no answer to her knock, went around to the shop he had built onto the garage. Sure enough, he was working there. He looked somehow pared down: his hair was cut shorter than usual, and his black shirt and pants made him seem thinner. Even the flesh of his face was reduced.

She invited him to eat supper with them every night, but he refused to accept unless she would let him pay them. After thinking about it a little, she agreed; Ral might object, but they could use the money, and it would be costly to feed another grown man. Besides, she knew Gavin wouldn't come otherwise.

She was about to leave when she saw a coffin standing up

in the corner of the shop. "Why, who did you make that for? Has a neighbor died?"

Gavin stopped and turned around, his back to his workbench, upon which he rested his hands. He smiled, then looked sober and said, "Dear Annie, I made it for you."

She looked at the coffin, her stomach doing a strange little shift to the side, then looked at him again.

He reached out and hugged her. His voice was thick: "At least I didn't lose you too." Then he let her go and smiled again. "Shall I sell it or store it? It's made just to your measure."

"Oh, sell it, sell it. I don't plan to use it for a long time." She shuddered at the thing again as she scurried out into the cool open air; it felt good on her burning cheeks.

She sang as she cooked that night, and all during supper she felt as if they were having a party because Gavin was there. He helped her with the dishes after supper. She protested at first, saying that he paid for his supper and shouldn't have to work for it too.

He said, "I pay for my share of the food, but I can at least help you with the dishes to thank you for the good cooking."

"It's no more work to cook for you; I have to cook for my own anyhow."

"Well, that may be, but if you won't let me help, I don't feel like I can be beholden to you for your work. I don't mind at all; I always helped my ma when I was at home. I was her last child, and she needed help. It made me feel good."

After that she didn't argue with him. They talked about growing up and the excitement of learning to do things.

146

Annie Bee started working for Dr. Baker again a couple of days a week. She had missed seeing the patients, and when she saw them, many of them told her that they were glad she was well and back again. They told her of their own hardships during the epidemic. Almost all had lost loved ones or friends. Many had lain too ill to sit by relatives who were dying in the same house; they had heard them cry for help and later not known whether they were dead or alive. Some had known others in the house were dead but had not had the strength to get help to bury them. Hundreds in the state had died.

The streets that she walked along seemed familiar, strangely like coming home after being home. She realized too that these patients had become part of her life. She had noticed things about their houses that she tried to copy in her own, and she had quit braiding her hair country-fashion, but like the women she saw put it in a topknot in the back and left it full and soft around the face. She had even begun to imitate the way Dr. Baker and their better-educated patients talked.

When she saw Reuben Quarles, she was shocked at how thin and weak he seemed. Leona said that he had had influenza and had almost died; she kept him on her lap for most of the visit. "My little stick-man's going to get better now, though. He's going to be big and strong so he can take care of me and his sisters. Ain't you, sweetheart?"

"Leona, if you don't mind my asking, what happened to his father?"

"No, that's all right, Annie Bee. It hurt a long time, but I've about got over it now. He got killed. He was a good man and a good father, but he had a temper, Lord, once that man saw red, couldn't nothing stop him. Some low-down, no-'count trash was messing around with his sister, and my Reuben— our boy here's named for him—told him to leave her alone, and he got some of his no-'count friends together and jumped Reuben one night, and 'stead of running, Reuben tried to fight them all. He made them mad enough one of them killed him with a knife."

Annie Bee put her hand over Leona's. "I'm so sorry."

"I still miss him, and I ain't like to find nobody good as he was and ain't going to settle for less. But we'll make it, long as I got my stick-man and Flora and Mabel." She squeezed the boy.

Annie Bee knew that somehow she would.

Every night Gavin would arrive just at suppertime. Ral would usually sit at the table talking with him until they finished the dishes. Then Gavin would stay to talk awhile, but he didn't stay late; all of them had to get up in the mornings.

While she mended or sewed and listened night after night, the men talked about the overtures for peace that the Germans were making. It seemed silly to Annie Bee; they had just gotten the powder plant built, and the war was going to end. Finally she asked what would happen to the plant.

"Well, probably they'll tear it down, unless they can find something else to do with it."

"And what about all the men working here? Ral, will you be out of work again?" Her curiosity had turned to concern.

Ral shrugged. "I don't know. It's just like crops; you never know whether you'll make a bushel of money or have to scrape to get by."

Annie Bee jabbed her needle into the pants she was patching. It seemed no matter what happened, she was at the mercy of something she couldn't control. How could God let such things happen to her?

Gavin said, "Reckon if the war ends, it'll change my plans some too. I'd thought maybe now that Mary's gone I'd enlist and go over there to tend the wounded. Only reason they didn't call me up before was that she depended on me.''

Annie Bee's heart lurched. It had been a pain to have Gavin eat her food and sit in her front room every night, then leave her to go to his own home. But not to see him at all would have been a worse pain, to wonder whether he was sick or well, dead or alive. She had of course worried about Nate. But Gavin! She thrust aside the thought that he had considered leaving her. And she silently thanked God for the peace that would keep him near her, to be seen some of the time.

IV. Truces

She began making the rounds four days a week again among Dr. Baker's patients, knowing that if Ral were to lose his job, she would need to have hers. There never seemed a lack of sick to tend at least. She thought that the children might protest her leaving, but they were glad to have their playmates at Prue's all the time again.

She was called back to the Lammingtons to help tend Roberta and her baby girl Amelia. It didn't take more than one hand to count the months since her marriage, but Annie Bee wasn't really surprised. The work was more interesting this time, for she was there during the daytime and saw everyone in the family. Everyone, that is, except for Mr. Lammington, who stayed in his room all the time; his diabetes made him afraid to do anything lest he be injured and not heal. Annie Bee also assumed from what Deborah and Willadene hinted that he was also drunk most of the time.

Victoria was large enough to produce a child of her own any minute, but Annie Bee saw that eating, not sleeping, was the cause of her weight. She usually went around carrying a box of Whitman's Samplers, and she sampled them until they were replaced with a new box. The new baby didn't promise to make her any happier, especially since her mother had not only accepted the child and the marriage, but anyone would have thought Mrs. Lammington had conceived and borne the whole family herself, she was so proud of it.

Emory was tall and slender with perfectly smoothed blond hair and a perfectly smooth chin. He was, so far as Annie Bee could tell, ornamental but not very functional. He spent his days wearing a path from the Lammingtons' to his parents' house three doors up the street, seeing what his momma thought about this and that, and whereas he usually held the baby the entire time company visited, he ignored her otherwise.

He also didn't spend much time with Roberta. Alicia, who was sixteen, was always asking him to play croquet with her or badminton or Chinese checkers. He usually did.

And at last Annie Bee got to see the enigmatic Wendell. One day just as she was coming up the front walk, a scrawny man of about forty counting some money passed her. His skin, mustache, and thinning hair all seemed the same dirty brown.

She asked Deborah, "Who was that leaving?"

Deborah looked around the empty hall. "That," she said, "was Mr. Phelps. He brings Mr. Horace his whiskey."

Annie Bee was considerably disappointed at the reality of Victoria's erstwhile lover.

Mr. McAfee was one of the more troublesome of Dr. Baker's patients. An old bachelor, he had some mysterious complaint that neither he nor Dr. Baker had told her about. It evidently didn't keep him from thinking of himself as cock of the walk; he leered at Annie Bee with his watery old eyes and sometimes made remarks that she ignored. She made sure she stayed well out of his reach, and she never mentioned his remarks to Ral, but one night she did give Ral and Gavin an account of her visit to him that afternoon. She had found him in bed, evidently in a bad way; he was moaning about going to meet his Maker. He asked her to get him some water so he could take one of the pills Dr. Baker had given him, and she found the envelope in the drawer he pointed out, unopened.

"I asked him why he hadn't been taking them, and he said, 'If it's the will of the Lord, I'll go, doctoring or not.' And I told him, 'It's the will of the Lord for me to come and make you take these pills.' And I told him he'd better take them regular so he didn't get in a shape like he was in again. Just like a baby—a man old as Pap that can't take care of hisself—himself no better'n Clara there."

Gavin and Ral laughed, and Gavin said, "Probably just wanted to be cajoled a little by a pretty woman, and don't have no faith in doctors nohow."

"Yeah, but he may be right, you know," Ral added. "When it's time to go, we're all going to go."

Annie Bee snorted. "If I walk out in front of a car coming down the road like a shot out of a gun, I'm going to go whether it's time or not. The Lord helps those that have the good sense to help themselves."

"Why, Annie, I thought you were the good Cumberland Presbyterian and Ral was one of those godless Methodists that don't know election and ain't like to. You all've lived together so long you're swapping views."

"Being elected don't mean you've got no call to use the sense God gave you. And He gave us all sense enough to come in out of the rain unless we decide we can't make our feet move."

"Well, as you told McAfee, maybe God sent you to make sure he did what his common sense should've told him to do in the first place."

The armistice did come, and Ral did lose his job, but he already had another, at least for the winter. Walter Huffines had told him that the coal company he worked for needed men to deliver to homes, and Walter and Gavin taught him how to drive. Shoveling the coal was dirty work, and he had to go over the river on the ferry to the city every day. But he liked being outside part of the time. And he became proud of handling the truck in the city traffic.

He drove his truck home one Saturday and took them into the city the next day. Annie Bee had to hold Nathan's hands at first to keep him from grabbing the steering wheel or one of the strange handles, but when they got into the city itself, they all were too busy looking at everything to notice the truck. Nathan pointed at every automobile, every truck, and every buggy he saw and said, "Car! Car!"

Ral drove them down Broadway, which was itself as wide as a cornfield, every inch cobbled. The buildings were two, three, even four stories above the street, fine buildings of stone or brick. People were coming out of churches that were grander than the courthouse in Ridgefield. Ral pointed out the Customs House and Union Station, and they stopped at the station and got out and went down to wait until a train pulled up at the sheds. Clara and Nathan were terrified and fascinated by the monster, and Annie Bee felt with them. Its size and the frightful noises that it made explained for her the havoc of the wreck the summer before when Dr. Baker had been gone for so long tending the injured. They all got cinders in their eyes.

She realized that Old Hickory was a crude new place, nothing like this. Then she thought how far above Ridgefield Old Hickory was, and how Stone's Creek with its small, rough houses would scarcely seem fit to live in to people in this splendid place.

One night when Ral came home, he marched straight into the kitchen, where Annie Bee was cooking dinner, without his usual romp with the children. Clara, outraged at this denial of her rights, followed and pulled on his pants leg. But he gave her no attention. "What do you mean, woman, letting that whore take care of our children?"

Fearing another slap, Annie Bee nevertheless turned to confront him. "I suppose you're talking about Prue. She's not a whore. She's married to Walter Huffines legal as you and me's married."

"You know what I mean. Walter said something today about Prue's first husband not even wanting to see their younguns, and like a fool I asked if he was still alive, and Walter said, 'Why sure, didn't Annie Bee tell you?' And I said, 'Oh, yeah, sure, reckon I forgot.' But you never told me nothing. How long you know about this?"

Annie Bee had meant to tell Ral, but at first she had needed to sort it out for herself. Later the right time never seemed to come, and finally she had just forgotten that she needed to tell him. Feeling her guilt now, she tried to explain why she had not told him, that she had found Prue a reliable, loving caretaker for Clara and Nathan, that she kept them clean, healthy, and happy. She added, "And she's divorced from McCartle in the eyes of the law."

Ral shook his head. "Annie Bee, the woman's left her husband and is living with another man. There's no law makes that right. She's a whore that ain't fitting to associate with you, much less innocent little children."

Clara, having tugged in vain, raised her voice. "Daddy! What's a whore?"

She must have been pleased with the results of this attempt, for both parents turned their attention wholly to her. But she didn't get the answer to her question. Her father just told her mother, "Now see what's happened because of you? Your child is learning filthy words."

"Well, she didn't learn it from me, or Prue either. If her father doesn't want her to learn bad words, he better not use them himself."

They ended the discussion till little ears were safely on pillows, but then Ral reopened it. He wanted Annie Bee to stop leaving the children with Prue, even if it meant quitting her job for Dr. Baker. Annie Bee adamantly refused to give Prue up as a friend or a baby-sitter; worst, she thought, was Ral's rejection of Prue while contending that Walter was a perfectly acceptable friend for him. She went to sleep reviewing all the injustices done women and knowing that he would not see any of them. She would not march with those unladylike suffragettes; politics was man's business. But she would not give up Prue either.

Dr. Baker had turned over most of his charity patients to Annie Bee, and one of these, Polly Probert, became close to her, almost like a mother. Somewhat crippled by a stroke on one side, Aunt Polly, as Annie Bee called her, nevertheless lived by herself in her old house, little more than a shack really, that even now stood on the edge of town and when it had been built must have been far out from any other dwelling. She had learned to walk on her crippled leg and could use her crippled arm to brace something against. She did not really need much medical attention. What she did need was able hands to help with getting her food and keeping her house together. She could no longer grow much in her garden, and the woods through which she had gone with her shotgun to pick off an occasional squirrel or rabbit had been cleared to build homes for the influx of factory workers. So Annie Bee often cooked a little extra and took it to Aunt Polly the next day. But she could not repair or halt the advancing decay of the old woman's house.

While telling Ral and Gavin about her visit to Aunt Polly's one day, Annie Bee mentioned that Aunt Polly searched the streets for discarded newspapers to stuff in the holes. Gavin offered to go some day to work on the house, and they agreed on a day for her to take him and introduce him.

That morning Gavin drove by to pick her up, the car packed with scrap lumber and tools. Since the closing of the powder plant, building in the town had completely stopped, so he had no work now except for the few small jobs he picked up and the furniture he made and sold in the city. Clara and Nathan went with their mother; she had taken them to visit Aunt Polly before, and the old woman in some measure replaced the grandmothers neither of them remembered.

They filled a vacancy for Aunt Polly too. She told Gavin that morning as she had told Annie Bee before of the three children she and her husband Tom had had and lost. Tom himself had died a young man, only thirty; since then she had lived alone.

"Seems like he made the sun rise, and when he went, there warn't much left for me," she said, looking at the hills to the east. "But a body's got to keep on going."

Annie Bee expected her words to remind Gavin of Mary, and she stole a look at him.

But to her surprise he was looking at her, almost searching her face, and it seemed to her as if he must read her love there.

Then it was he who looked down.

Later as she held a board for him to nail, he accidentally put his hand down on top of hers; his flew off as though he had touched hot iron.

On the way home, he made small talk, but it was only the children who replied. She couldn't pretend that she had not seen his look and surmised his understanding. She felt as if she were pregnant: what she carried inside her was heavy but living, and if it came to light, it would bring great joy and great pain.

She worried about his coming to supper that night. She knew that he would say nothing about her to Ral; he had never been cruel or even unfeeling to any soul as long as she had known him. He might have such contempt for her sinful love that he would not come ever again. That would be no worse than she deserved, and she braced herself to bear such emptiness. The best that she hoped for was that he would ignore her guilt.

And that was what happened. He arrived a little later than usual, well after Ral came home, and spent all his conversation on Ral. He and she did not look at each other when they exchanged platters and bowls at the table, and as they did the dishes, he faced Ral all the time except when he was taking a dish out of the scalding pan to dry. He excused himself right after the dishes were finished, saying that he was working on some furniture that he wanted to finish and varnish that night.

She was grateful. He saw her sin but was forgiving it.

Gradually their relationship resumed its old form. But always now she controlled herself: she dared not study his face in the lamplight or join in his teasing of the children. All she hoped was to continue to be able sometimes to know he was in the same room where she could hear him.

V. Reunion and Separation

She was trudging home one day after making her rounds when she saw a strange man carrying a worn valise on her porch, looking through the window. Her heart in her throat, she didn't know whether to yell and scare him off or to run and get help.

Then the man turned and saw her. He started down the steps, hanging on to the porch post, and then limped down the walk.

She started to turn and run but stopped; something seemed familiar about him. Then she ran toward him as fast as she could. "Nate! Nate! It's you!"

He picked her up and swung her around as if she were a schoolgirl. Then they kissed each other and both began chattering at the same time. She said, "Wait! I have to get something first!" And she dashed off to Prue's.

He knelt down and reached out for Clara as soon as she ran

out the Huffines' door calling "Uncle Nate!" But when she got almost to him, she stopped, put her finger in her mouth, and turned back to look for her mother. "Uncle Nate" had become a name for the letters the mailman brought; this stranger had no claim on her.

Annie Bee watched him try to woo her, but when she saw that he was not going to win easily, she called his attention to his namesake, whom she was carrying. There was no obstacle there; Nathan would have gone to Kaiser Wilhelm himself if that fleeing monarch had turned up on their street and held out his arms.

As soon as Clara saw that her brother was getting all the attention, she decided that it was safe to talk with this suddenly embodied letter-writer.

The first hour was taken up with Annie Bee's cooking supper and trying to talk with Nate while the children, completely won over with candy from Uncle Nate's valise, eagerly sought other pleasures from him. Finally, worn out with piggyback rides, tosses into the air, trotting horses, and songs, Uncle Nate collapsed laughing on the couch and became just a new human to climb over.

Then Ral came home, followed almost at once by Gavin, and the shouts and surprises and hugs started all over again.

After supper the children went to bed and the grown-ups settled down to talk. Nate gave Annie Bee a pink silk handkerchief, thin as the dried petal of a poppy, edged with lace and embroidered in silk with violets and the word *Sister*. He gave Ral a little box. "Them's some playing cards I got over there. They're not quite like what we've got."

Annie Bee reached to see them, but Nate quickly grabbed her hand and said, "No, womenfolk wouldn't be interested in such as that." He grinned at the men.

He told about the trip over in a British transport ship. "Them Tommies speak English, but it sounds so different I couldn't understand a word they said for the first week. And they was always saying *we* talked funny. Ain't that the beatingest? Then we got to France, and the Frogs have a whole different way of talking altogether."

"Did you learn them English?" Ral asked.

"No, there was a lot more of them than there was of me. Half the time I didn't see more'n half a dozen Americans in a day. Now that was at the first; later on there was more Americans come, 'Yanks' we was all called, whether we was from the North or the South, and I reckon the most of them come about the time I got wounded."

They asked about the fighting, and he shook his head. "That's nothing to talk about. That's living in a hole in the ground, full of water half the time, cold as Hell in the winter and hot as Hell in the summer, chasing the rats out sometimes and trying to catch them for dinner the rest. It's not the shooting and the gas that's so awful; it's the trenches. Why, half the men that died, the Germans didn't kill them, it was sickness. Lord, Lord, I hope I never have to be in a place like that again."

Gavin asked, "Was you in the trenches the whole time till you got hurt?"

"No, they started me in on working on motors, and that was a whole lot better. I liked that. They had me back at headquarters working on the trucks and cars, and then they moved me to wherever they was flying from, and I worked on airplanes. That was the best. I'd like to do that all the time— work on those machines and see them go up in the air and know that they couldn't do it without me."

Annie Bee asked what the prettiest thing he had seen was.

"Well, excepting some of the girls and New York when we was coming back, the country there. They've got pretty little whitewashed houses with straw on the roof set out in the middle of the prettiest rolling fields you ever seen, not a rock in them, though they've got some rock fences. Almost enough to make a man like farming. And they've got some churches like Heaven itself, all cold gray stone with these great big blue-and-red windows made into pictures and statues of Mary and Jesus and saints all over the place and carvings all over the posts and funny little stone critters peering out at you just where you don't expect them. They make you feel like some wicked old stepmother in one of the old stories Mammy used to tell has trapped a lot of monsters out of everybody's dreams and turned them all into stone.''

Annie Bee sniffed. ''All Papist doings! I bet some of those pretty girls you were talking about served the woman on the scarlet beast with seven horns too!''

Nate grinned. ''Well, they served a good many. Or a good many served them.'' The men laughed.

Annie Bee ignored that. ''And the filth? Wasn't—weren't they all covered with filth?''

''Oh, I saw plenty of dirty people all right, but no more'n here. And the food! I tell you, those people never heard of cornbread, but they can fix raw meat so good you don't ever want to cook it no more. They put all these different kinds of gravy over ever'thing so you don't know what's under them, but you don't care. And they can beat up eggs—just plain old ordinary eggs—so they taste better'n any eggs you ever had before.''

''Well, maybe so, but I bet I wouldn't eat nothing there unless I saw the hands of them that cooked it and they were scrubbed clean before they touched my food. And you wouldn't catch me eating raw meat, gravy or no. Why, that's scarcely human.''

Annie Bee went to bed wondering that her own brother, who grew up eating their own mother's good cooking, could even talk about such heathenish ways.

She and Ral had thought at first that Nate had come to Old Hickory before going home, but the next morning as she cleaned up after breakfast and they talked, she learned that he had been at Stone's Creek for a week before he came to see them. He had told Callie Jane not to call Gavin; he wanted to surprise them. So she caught up on news of all the Cutterfields.

Then she asked, ''Why didn't you bring Leathie with you? Is she sick?''

"No, no, she's all right." He frowned and said, "Annie Bee, I came here partly to ask a favor of you. I wish you'd talk to Leathie and put some sense in her head."

"Why, Nate Cutterfield, I've knowed—known Leathie almost as long as I can remember you, and I never noticed her having much less sense than you have."

"Well, she does now. I've been trying to get her to leave that little hick town up ten miles past nowhere, and she won't hear of it. It's not taking care of her pappy, neither. Molly Lou and Lusetta's surely enough to take care of one old half-crazy man that don't do nothing but sit by the fireplace like an animal in its den winter and summer. She just don't want to change.

"But I don't intend to spend the rest of my life stuck up there plowing and sowing and plowing and reaping. I want to travel—go all over the world and see places. You know how we used to climb up in the trees and look out over the tops and pretend we was on ships going to Japan and India and all kinds of places? Well, I done some of that for real when I went to the war. And I want to see the rest of the world—all of it. I learned enough about motors and planes to find a job wherever we go—long as it's not some place in the hills where they wait all day just to see a car go by. I'm not going to live forever, and while I live, I want to try ever' new thing I can. And she just wants to set in Stone's Creek on some godforsaken farm."

"Maybe she wants to sit there with some babies—your babies. You ever think of that?"

"Yeah. But I don't care about having babies. I'm enough for her to tend to." He grinned, satisfied with that at least. "And that's not all of it. Suppose she says yeah, she'll leave her cook-stove and garden patch and travel with me. She's just a country girl—don't know how to dress, don't know how to talk, ain't likely to learn. Why, look at you, Annie Bee; you're not the same little hick you was two years ago when I left. You've changed like me. Your skirts don't drag the ground no more. And you talk more like city folks now."

She knew that it was true, and she was glad that he had noticed. But then she thought of Leathie, dear Leathie, with her clear, open look. "Well, anyhow, you love her, don't you? That's the main thing. You can work it out, can't you?"

Nate looked out the window. "I don't know. I just don't know, Annie Bee."

As he watched her cook dinner, he patted her hair and said, "You're the only one of us got Mammy's hair—black as a blackbird's wing. You ought to get it cut short like feathers; lots of girls in Europe do now."

"Why, Nate, you know it's a shame for a woman to cut her hair. The Bible says so."

"It must be a lot of trouble to take care of so long. And when it's short, it feels soft like fur in a man's hand."

"Man's meant to be of few days and full of troubles. Woman too. And your hand's got no place in nobody's hair but Leathie's."

A shrug and a wry look were his only response.

That afternoon he left; he said he wanted to visit some friends he had met in France who lived in Nashville.

That night after Gavin had left and the children were in bed, she told Ral about the disturbing things Nate had said. "He ought not run off and leave Leathie like this and talk about her that way. He's to blame if anything goes wrong between them."

"Blame?" Ral said. "Nate's not perfect—nobody is. Leathie's not either. Sometimes things go wrong and nobody's to blame."

"Well, maybe nobody's perfect, but if Nate wanted to, he could come a whole lot closer than he is." She drew her mouth into a firm line.

Ral made no response.

164

That night she dreamed about Mammy. She was trying to call Mammy to tell her about Nate's trouble with Leathie and her own love for Gavin. But the telephone turned into a paper bag in her hand. And then, wonder of wonders, Mammy was there anyhow; she had heard and understood, even when Annie Bee had talked into a paper bag. And Mammy was young and strong again, with no white in her hair, walking through the fields as Annie Bee had seen her do a hundred times to catch a baby in her white apron. And Annie Bee was a woman grown, but Mammy was holding her hand.

When Annie Bee woke up, she was sorry that it was only a dream. But she also felt comforted that she had seen Mammy again. And that she was young.

A few days later Dr. Baker's secretary gave Annie Bee a message to come by Leona's. She had missed their usual Thursday because of Nate's visit, and Leona had promised her some flower bulbs to plant for the next spring, so she figured that they were dug up. But when she approached the house, she saw a black ribbon on the door and remembered Reuben's pinched little face the last time that she had seen him.

Inside there were two old women, a girl about twelve, and an old man, all black, sitting in the small room with Leona, Flora, and Mabel. They were looking at a small wooden coffin on the bed. She hugged Leona when she came in; neither could talk. Finally she said, "I'm sorry."

Leona nodded. Then she introduced Annie Bee to the others, and they all nodded and greeted each other. She offered Annie Bee some coffee and a piece of poundcake someone had brought.

"Was it the asthma?"

Leona nodded again. "He got a cold, and it kept getting worse and worse. He was short of breath all the time. It would hurt him just to breathe in or out. And then he got this awful cough that just wore him down." She wiped her eyes and nose with a handkerchief. "Toward the end he was just too tired to breathe any more. But he went in his sleep."

"Why didn't you let me know sooner? I'd have sat up with him."

"Dr. Baker did finally come. I told the woman at his office I was going to bring Reuben and sit on his front steps till the doctor would see him if he didn't, so he come. But it was too late; the doctor said it was into pneumonia, and it warn't nothing he could do." She broke down then. "My son! My only son!"

Annie Bee, thinking of her own Nathan as well as her friend, held her until she had stopped crying and blown her nose.

Leona said, "I thank you for coming; I know you've got other people you've got to see today."

"Yes, but I'll be back tonight."

And she was. She cooked double and packed half in a box to take and left as soon as supper was over; Gavin insisted that he could do the dishes by himself, and Ral drove her over in the company truck, albeit with some grumbling. She sat up with Leona and some of her neighbors until midnight, when Ral came to get her.

The next day she went to the funeral. She had never been to a black funeral before, and she was the only white person there, but it didn't seem all that different from the white funerals she had been to.

The preacher spoke about the story where King David had banished Absalom for killing his brother Amnon, and Nathan the prophet had sent a woman to talk to David. She pretended to have a similar son and to want to know whether to forgive him, and when the king said that she should, she told him that he should treat his own son as he had told her to treat hers.

Annie Bee had heard and read the story before, of course; but the text kept running through her mind: "For we must needs die, and are as water spilt on the ground, which cannot be gathered up again." She saw Leona's tear-streaked face and steady eyes. That was the first time that she had realized her friend was beautiful.

She was called to the Lammingtons again for night duty. Dr. Baker did not instruct her himself, but left a message that she was to see Victoria for instructions.

Wondering why Miss Mamie was not directing her, she learned when she met Victoria, who must have weighed two hundred pounds by then, that Miss Mamie was the patient—or one of them, at least. Victoria told her that Miss Mamie and Roberta were both suffering from nervous prostration and that Alicia had "other problems." "You will need to care for Alicia as you did for me, and I trust that you will be as silent now as you have been in the past. If we find that you have not, we shall certainly never employ you again and shall attempt to persuade Dr. Baker that he should not either."

"It's none of my business to talk about yours," Annie Bee said. She restrained her curiosity.

"I'm glad you know that. Now because there are so many to watch, we'll pay you double what we have before. But all three have been given strong sedatives, so Dr. Baker says you shouldn't really have much to do except take care of Mother and Roberta when the sedatives wear off and change Alicia's dressings and make sure she doesn't develop a fever. Dr. Baker has new sedatives with instructions in each room. I trust that double the usual wages is enough?"

"Yes, that's fine." Annie Bee was glad that there would be more work to relieve the boredom.

"Now, because I know you'll hear from that gossipy Deborah or Willadene anyhow and you might as well get it straight, I'll tell you what's happened. My sister Roberta's perfect husband has added Alicia to his harem, and she's just lost his child." Victoria seemed almost smug as she said that. "Roberta and Mother are understandably upset, although I could have told them from personal experience that he was willing to be unfaithful to Roberta. Of course, I rejected his advances completely. And now he's been turned out of the house forever."

Sitting in the stifling rooms that smelled of perfume and sweat, Annie Bee wondered if that was a punishment.

VI. Lost Battles

Mrs. Thorburn was one of the worryingest of Dr. Baker's patients. It wasn't that she worried others; it was that she worried about herself all the time that she was pregnant and about her baby all the time after she was born. Maybe it was because it was her first.

At any rate, when the baby developed a rash, it was almost more than she could stand. She fretted from the time Annie Bee arrived till time for her to leave, although Annie Bee had assured her that she would make certain that Dr. Baker came to check the baby as soon as he could.

"When's that like to be?" she asked.

"Well, it might be tomorrow or maybe the day after. I'll let him know soon as I can."

"I just don't know what I'll do till he comes. Isn't there something you know that'll help poor little Bonnie till he sees her?"

Annie Bee felt uneasy. This was the very thing Dr. Baker

had told her from the first not to do. But the truth was that she had known the moment she saw the baby that her rash was of the sort her mother had treated with common ground-ivy tea. Clara had had it herself once, and it had cleared right up after a couple of feedings with the tea. Mrs. Thorburn's eyes beseeched her. So she gathered a few handfuls of the plant from the yard, brewed some tea for the first feeding, and gave instructions for the next.

Three days later Dr. Baker's car stopped in front of the house they rented, and he marched to the door swinging his cane rather than leaning on it. His message was short and to the point: she had disobeyed his expressed orders, and he had no further wish for her services.

When she told Ral that night after Gavin left, his response surprised her. He did not regret the loss of the money, even though his job delivering coal might well end as soon as the weather grew warmer and the company laid off drivers. He told her, "You shouldn't've done it—doctoring's man's work." Then he added, "Reckon you won't have no call now to leave your younguns with that . . . woman." He smiled as if he had won something.

Annie Bee made no response, but she felt the anger build inside her. It seemed she was in the wrong about everything. She went to bed right away and feigned sleep when Ral retired; at least, she would not participate in any celebration of her own defeat.

170

The next morning she defiantly left the children with Prue despite the expense and went to Gavin's workshop on the chance that he would be there. He was, and he brought out a chair for her and sat down himself while she told him of her loss.

"Do you all need money? I could lend you some," he said.

"Oh, no, we've saved some. It's not that. It's just hard to know that Dr. Baker thinks I'm not fitting to take care of people."

"Well, you've got to look at it his way, Annie. He's the one responsible, and even though you and me know your maw was as good as a doctor, he don't know that. He's just afraid something would go wrong, and folks would blame him."

She got up and began pacing back and forth, arms folded across her breast, head down, as she complained: "You're no more help than Ral."

He frowned and looked down himself. "Ral's the one you ought to go to."

She stopped with her back to him. "Ral doesn't give me anything when I do go to him. You always gave to Mary."

He got up and turned to his workbench. "She was my wife. You're Ral's wife."

Annie Bee felt guilt and despair. "I'm sorry." Her voice came out a whisper, so she tried to steady it before she went on. "I didn't mean to make you grieve. I'll leave you alone."

Tears blinding her eyes, she started putting on her coat, but he caught her by the shoulders, pulled her close, and kissed her. "Oh, Annie, Annie," he said, kissing her face and lips again and again. Then he released her, his face lit. "Go home, my sweet. Go home now." He stood with his hands behind his back and watched while she put on her coat, picked up her pocketbook, and obeyed like one hypnotized.

She didn't go home right away. She walked through the raw February day, the memory of his kisses warming her face, without a conscious direction. She found herself near Aunt Polly's but didn't stop to visit; she had to be alone with the fullness of her heart. She walked past the town out into the country, her steps light in the cloying mud.

She stopped when she reached the woods. The last snow, shaded by only the bare limbs, still patched the ground. She sat on an outcropping on the hill where freezing water had pocked the gray limestone and runoff had worn it smooth.

She looked at the trees around her, the dogwoods swollen with spring buds, the maples and other hardwoods showing no leaf but only the color under the bark and at the buds like a blush. And the cedars, that had lost their winter blackness, their flat deadness, were again green, living trees, spreading out into space, breathing, reaching. Soon they would be red at the tips, then pale with new growth, exposed to the sun and the wind and the chill spring rains.

She was calm that night. She knew before he said it that Gavin would not come again to eat with them. What he said didn't matter, that he was not selling all the furniture he made at home and was taking a job building houses in Nashville and would not have time what with driving back and forth to eat with them each night.

She did not join Ral's expostulations until his wondering look reminded her of her role as concerned sister-in-law. Then she could look at Gavin calmly and even smile as she told him she would miss his help with the dishes if he quit coming. She knew of course that protests would not affect his decision.

Her calmness sprang from her knowledge that the best and the worst had happened and all the rest was inevitable. He knew her love, yes, and shared it. Now the only paths open to them led them away from each other. But she could bear that separation because of the knowledge that necessitated it. Always, always, she could carry the knowledge that Gavin had loved her. Nothing better could come.

The next morning, in the cupboard shelf where Gavin had put her skillets, she found a note from him: "Dear Annie, I want to see you but better not. Thank you, dear girl. Yours, Gavin." She first put the note in her Bible, then moved it to her unused nurse's bag.

In the days that followed, she thought over and over of their last meeting alone. She understood what Gavin had said about Dr. Baker—that she had not thought of his point of view when he fired her but only of her own. And of course that was what she had done toward Gavin too: she had not seen his actions as coming from himself but only as reflections of her own. She thought again of the hidden lives of others that she had glimpsed at her mother's funeral. How long had she been sealed in herself and not seen that Gavin too had hidden, hidden his feelings for her?

The days were empty except for the children and her household chores. For a while she took pleasure in cooking more, cleaning more often, and visiting with Prue and Aunt Polly. She made a dress for Clara and embroidered it lavishly. She went walking with the children, but they were too small to take as far as the hill as long as the spring air was still chilly.

The children missed playing with the McCartles and Huffines all the time, but Annie Bee used some of the time to try to teach them, Clara at least. Prue had taught them to count, but she didn't know how to read herself. Annie Bee began teaching Clara the alphabet, then simple words. She would write a line and have Clara copy it. She wrote out "Three Little Pigs," one of Clara's favorite stories, and Clara learned to read it all. She wore out the copybook from carrying it around all the time.

Sometimes they clashed too. One afternoon Clara and Nathan had been riding their "horsies," sticks that Annie Bee had tied a string to for reins, when a storm came up. Annie Bee called them to come in, but Clara said, "Wait till I get my horsie. It's down by the fence."

"I said for you to come in now. You're going to get wet."

"And I said I was going to get my horsie." She stamped her foot and ran to the fence.

When Annie Bee caught her, she switched her legs with a willow. But Clara had her horsie.

Annie Bee told Prue about it the next day. "I declare, I don't know where she gets her stubbornness."

Prue didn't say anything.

Sometimes Annie Bee wondered if Dr. Baker had dismissed her because he feared that she would take some of his patients away from him herself. At other times she thought that her boredom was a punishment from the Lord for her guilty love.

Often after supper Ral would now go to talk with Walter as he had grown used to talking with Gavin. She would sit alone sewing until he returned; the children were in bed, nor did she and Prue visit each other when Ral was at home. So she was alone with her thoughts. They were usually memories or dreams of Gavin.

When Ral wanted to make love, she always gave herself to him. But she imagined that it was Gavin that she held.

One March evening just when the crocuses were dying and the daffodils were beginning to bloom, storm clouds hid the moon. The wind bent the trees and banged the shutters, a cold, lonesome sound. After she finished the dishes, she went outside and sat on the back stoop with her mending despite the thunder, waiting for the storm to begin. The flash of distant heat lightning turned into closer bolts, and then the rain started pouring down in sheets so fast that she got wet before she could gather up her things and get inside.

That night she lay awake listening to the thunder and knowing what she would do.

After Ral left for work in the morning, she took the children to Prue and asked her to keep them for the day. Then she started picking her way through the mud to Gavin's house, rehearsing what she would say: "I came because I want you. If you want me, take me. If you don't, send me away." She knew that the new job he had told them about was just an excuse to keep from seeing her every night; she didn't for a minute believe that he wouldn't be there, working in his shop.

And he was there. He opened the door and stepped back to let her in, too startled to say anything at first.

She started, "I came . . . ," but she couldn't finish. She moved toward him like letting go of the grapevine on the bluff and falling toward the swimming hole, anticipating and dreading the shock of the chill water on her body. But this seemed slower than a fall, slow enough that she noticed a gash on his left hand as he reached for her. She raised her eyes to the light in his face. Meeting him was like the fulfillment of smooth water bearing her up.

Wordless but still holding her around the shoulders, he led her to the house and into his bedroom.

She knew that they would be together only this once and that it would be over before it seemed real, so she tried to remember each motion, each word, to keep for the rest of her life. Like the waves of love that washed through her, the ripples must circle out forever, fainter and fainter, but always centered on this meeting.

He started to withdraw before he came, but she whispered "No" and locked her hands behind his back. Afterward, lying on his arm in his warm, soft bed, she felt as if she were thawing after the frozen months. He was a fire for her to warm herself by.

Book Four

The Pain of Finite Hearts

1919

I. Guilt

When she left Gavin this time, she knew where she was going—to the hill beyond Aunt Polly's. She had to be alone.

But as she sat listening to the birds and looking at the green blades of grass and the swelling leaf buds, she knew that she could not be alone enough, for she wanted to get away from herself—her own mind—too. She wondered if that was what happened when people went out of their minds: they were trying to get away from something in themselves that they couldn't bear, so they left their own minds.

At any rate, being alone didn't relieve her loss or her guilt.

On the other hand, there was no one else to turn to. If only her mother had been alive, she could have told her; her mother would still love her no matter what she did. But she couldn't talk to anyone else. Telling Gavin how she felt would add to his own guilt. Telling Ral would hurt him so deeply that she could never forgive herself that hurt, even if he could understand and forgive her unfaithfulness.

She realized that this one act had tipped the balance to him now. Whatever lacks he had been responsible for in their marriage before were now dwarfed by her unfaithfulness. She had sinned against the laws of God and man, but mostly she had sinned against him. How could she face him again? She hid her face in her hands so that not even the sun could see her.

She wished for Leathie to talk to, then realized that even Leathie could not hear her without condemnation. It was Leathie's own brother that she had hurt, the brother who had made them sisters, the brother whom Annie Bee had insisted on marrying, had chosen out of all the world to claim.

Well, he was hers now.

And to think that she had condemned Nate for wanting something different in life from what Leathie wanted. As far as she knew, Nate had never been unfaithful to Leathie. And if he had, thousands of miles away from his wife in France, what did that prove but that he was truly her own brother?

Prue had been honester. Prue had gone to her husband and told him that she wanted another man. So Ral called Prue a whore. What, then, was she? She would be ashamed to tell even Prue, whom she had always felt superior to before.

And Gavin himself. Had she really been fair to him? She had forced herself upon him, gone to him in such a way that he couldn't refuse her without hurting her. Maybe he hadn't really wanted her.

That thought tortured her the most.

When she stopped to get the children, Prue said, "Your brother-in-law come to see you while you was gone. I saw him come out the back door and look around for you, so I told him you was gone and asked him if he wanted me to tell you

180

anything, and he said no, he was just in the neighborhood and stopped by. Then he went on back into the house.''

Annie Bee thanked her for the message and started to pay her for keeping the children.

Prue protested, saying that she wouldn't take anything from Annie Bee now that she wasn't taking any money in from nursing.

Annie Bee said, ''Then I'll keep your children for you sometime.''

But Prue just smiled and said, ''Where would I go without the younguns? I ain't got no friends but you to visit, you know.''

That was too much for Annie Bee, and she began crying. She knew that it was not for Prue but for herself, and shame at her own selfishness made her control herself as soon as she could. She told Prue that she wasn't feeling well, which brought on new offers of help that she didn't want, but she finally extricated herself from her well-meaning friend and took her children home.

After adding the wrongs that she had done Clara and Nathan to her list, Annie Bee thought of Gavin. Why had he come by? Did he want to tell her not to see him again? Or . . . ? She could not finish the question to herself.

She was cooking cornbread to use for hen-and-dressing, Ral's favorite dinner, when she got a partial answer. In the skillets in her cupboard where Gavin had left his note before, she found another. All it said was ''Dearest Annie, I'll always remember but you must forget. Thank you. Love, Gavin.''

Crying again, she put it in her nurse's bag with the other note.

The rest of the day she spent trying to figure out why he had written it. Its very politeness made it sound final, like a farewell. And hadn't that been what the first note had been too? Hadn't she disregarded what he had asked her before so that now he was telling her as clearly as he could without hurting her that he didn't want her?

Or was he thinking of her and trying to give her life back

to her? Didn't he know that that was the last thing she wanted now? Whatever she wanted.

She wanted to pray for forgiveness, but she knew that she was not sorry, not truly sorry, no matter what. It was that realization that steeled her to face Ral and make the evening outwardly at least like all the others that they had shared.

That night as she tried to go to sleep and tried even harder not to awaken Ral, she began to worry about being pregnant. She couldn't decide even whether it would be good or bad if she were. Ral would think that the child was his; certainly there was always a chance of that, although he had kept his word after his mother's illness and had never tried even to persuade her to have more children. And she and Gavin would wonder.

Or the child would form an open breach. Gavin would claim it and her, and they would be the family she had dreamed of. Mary had never given him children. But what then of Ral? And Clara and Nathan? Would Ral let her keep the children? Or would he take them to be brought up by Molly Lou? Or by some faceless stepmother?

In the morning she wrote an answer to Gavin's letter: "Dearest Gavin, I'll never forget. Love always, Annie." She had thought of many longer answers, but they contradicted each other. And this at least she knew was true. She wrote his full name on the envelope and told the children that they were going for a walk. Hoping that he was in the shop, she knocked at the house and, when he didn't answer, slid the envelope under his front door. Whatever happened now, she would do no more.

Dr. Baker came to see her the next week. After some aimless preliminaries, he asked her to return to work for him. "I was hasty and scarcely polite. Surely one error of judgment should not outweigh your excellent record while working for me."

"Oh, Dr. Baker, thank you. I know I shouldn't have done it, and I promise I never will again. I'd like to go back to nursing."

"Well, the patients miss you. And I've missed you too." He cleared his throat. "After all, they can't expect me to do it all without some help. But remember, no prescribing!"

After her second contrite promise, they set up arrangements for her beginning again. Annie Bee welcomed the work not so much for the money as for something to fill her days and her thoughts.

A week later she knew that she was not pregnant. This meeting that had wrecked her soul would not disrupt her outward life. She saw the red smear with equal relief and regret, and she remembered how Maude had resorbed her foal: what had been between her and Gavin would be no more, except for the memory.

Nate, alone again, came to visit them just before Ral turned thirty in April.

Remembering the party that Mary had given for Gavin's thirtieth birthday, Ral suggested that they invite Gavin to celebrate his, which was on a Sunday.

With a pounding heart, Annie Bee agreed, and Ral went to ask him. But Gavin pleaded work on a house that had to be finished. So the three of them and the children ate birthday dinner without him.

Afterward Nate wanted to go to Nashville to see his friends again, and Ral offered to let him drive the coal truck. But the road was muddy, and when Nate started up, he got stuck. Walter and Prue weren't at home, so Nate tried to push while Ral drove. But they just dug deeper ruts.

Annie Bee offered to help, and they laughed.

Then Gavin came by to wish Ral a happy birthday, so he helped Nate push, but they did no better.

Finally, Ral got out and said, "Well, I see you've got to have some real muscle back here. Gavin, you take over the wheel and let a younger man show you how it's done."

Annie Bee looked at Ral, but he was grinning. Gavin swapped places with him, and Ral and Nate did get the truck out, although Annie Bee told herself that it was because Gavin knew how to drive the truck better than Ral.

She saw that Gavin would have left as soon as they got the truck going except that it would have seemed strange to refuse Ral's invitation to come in and wash the mud off. So while Ral gave directions to Nate, Gavin followed Annie Bee into the house.

Neither spoke as she poured water from the teakettle into the washbasin. She had gone out into the mild April air without her lace collar on, but now the back of her bare neck felt cold, exposed to his gaze as she bent her head to aim the stream of warm water.

Then, as he was washing his hands and she was refilling the kettle from the bucket with her back again turned toward him, he said, "Annie, I got no right, but I want you to come again. If you don't want to, that's all right."

Turning, she couldn't answer. She had not known until then how heavy had been her fear that she had burdened him with love that he hadn't wanted.

He read her answer in her face and smiled.

As always, his smile pulled at her heart and made her smile too. But she heard Ral coming in the front door, so she just nodded quickly.

Nate told her the next day that he wanted to divorce Leathie. "I've got a little girl in Nashville that's worth two of her," he added defiantly.

A month before Annie Bee would have driven her brother from the house for saying something like that. Now she bent her head and just said, "Leathie's been a good, true wife to you, Nate. You know she never loved anybody else."

"She's never had nobody else to pay her attention. Look, it's for her too I want to be free. We don't make each other happy no more. All we do when we're together is fight. I'm not the same as I was before I went away. I'm sorry, but I'm just no good for her no more. She'd be happier with some dirt farmer that never saw nothing prettier'n the back end of a mule."

"Now, Nate, you know she'll never marry nobody else. Look at Molly Lou; she never married because of a week of marriage to a man she hardly knew."

"What she does is up to her. Have I got to be miserable the rest of my life because of her notions?"

"Who's the girl in Nashville?"

It was his turn to bend his head down. "She's a nurse I met in the hospital in France. Name's Amy Kay Tucker. A real educated girl—come over with a bunch of doctors from Vanderbilt. I was surprised she'd even look at a hick like me."

They sat at the kitchen table while he told her about meeting Amy Kay, first when he had been gassed and again when his leg had been shot. "Ain't that the beatingest? Out of all the soldiers and nurses in France, we was put together both times. It seemed like we was just meant to be together."

"Now, Nate, you can't mean that it was the Lord's will for you to fall in love with somebody besides your wife."

"The Lord's or the Devil's, it happened." He looked defiantly at her.

She saw through his bravado that he was in love with this

city girl and that he was as bewildered and unhappy as she was. She wondered if Nate and Amy Kay had made love in France and if they did now when Nate went into Nashville to visit his "friends."

Well, she wouldn't be the one to cast a stone. She put her hand over his and said, "I hope you do the right thing."

He grinned, the old mischief coming out again. "And what's that, Saint Annie Bee?"

She smiled herself. "You came to the wrong person to ask that, brother." But she didn't tell him how wrong she now was.

II. Fruits

She went to Gavin as soon as she could arrange to be away from home and her patients without suspicion. They were shyer with each other than they had been the first time, but afterward, they talked more.

Gavin said, "You know I've always loved you one way or another. When Sally married Cleavus, you became the little sister I always wanted."

"Oh, yes, I know that. You always teased me just like a brother—remember how I hated for you to go on about my freckles?"

He pushed back the sheet and bent to kiss the skin above her breasts. "And they really do go clear to Z." He pillowed his head there while she tangled her fingers in the ringlets of his hair.

"You were my big brother too. But all at once I stopped thinking of you like that and wished . . . you were something else."

"When did that happen?" His words were lazy, content.

She remembered Mary's sickroom and his smile, but she answered, "Oh, I don't know—after we moved down here."

He raised his head and looked at her. "I remember the first time I knew I loved you as a woman. It was when you saw your coffin that I had made, and you looked at me like if I said 'Die' you'd have to, and I knew then that I couldn't bear to lose you, that it would be worse than losing Mary because I always knew she was going, but you had to go on looking at me with your chin turned up and your eyes so blue they're black."

She kissed his forehead and slowly wound a curl of his hair around her finger. "I loved you before then. I loved you while Mary was still alive." She closed her eyes to keep from having to see his reaction.

He kissed her mouth. "You never hurt her." He leaned to the side, bent his arm, and propped his head on his hand. "The first time I thought you loved me was that day at Aunt Polly's when she talked about her husband and I saw the way you looked at me. I knew then that you were like to be hurt, and I thought I'd stay away. But that night you seemed so far away I decided I'd imagined it, and I thought it couldn't hurt for me to see you like a friend, that you couldn't care about an old fool like me."

"I thought you despised me for . . . for wanting you. And then when you kissed me, I thought that would be enough— just knowing you did care about me, even a little. But it wasn't. I just kept wanting you more and more."

"I only wanted not to hurt you, but no matter what I did, I couldn't help but hurt you."

She closed her eyes. "The only thing that hurts me is to have to leave you."

He lay back on the pillow and didn't speak for so long that she was beginning to think he was going to sleep when he said, "Would you leave Ral for me?"

She thought about her answer. "I don't know. I don't know if I could tell him."

188

They lay looking at each other, not knowing what to do when they left their sunlit room.

Rumors filled Old Hickory again—that the DuPont company was going to buy back the powder plant and make it a rayon and cellophane factory and more people would be hired than had worked there during the war. It was sure that the government was selling the whole town; there were signs up all around offering it for sale.

And a bridge, a huge steel suspension bridge, was being built over the river to connect the town to Nashville. Ral and Walter still used the ferry to go to work every day, but they talked about how much faster it would be to drive into the city when the bridge was built.

Ral talked to Annie Bee about whether he ought to apply for work at the new plant or keep on working for the coal company. He hadn't been laid off when deliveries were cut back by warm weather, and he liked the men he worked with. But wages had been higher at the powder plant. "We could get a place of our own sooner if I worked at the plant. Long as the job lasted, anyhow." He paced back and forth in the kitchen.

Annie Bee was peeling potatoes. "Well, wash-silk—rayon—dresses are what most women are wearing now for Sunday best. They seem kind of flashy to me, and I'm not sure rayon wears well."

"Nothing's as good as the homespun Ma used to make. I've wore my good dark blue wool suit she made for—it must be fifteen years now."

She looked at him, surprised. It was the first time he had mentioned his mother since she died. "What work would you rather do, drive or work at the plant?"

He shrugged his shoulders. "Don't matter much. Whatever I get paid most for, I reckon. Then when I get enough, we can leave this town for good and have us a farm again." He was standing with his hands in his pants pockets, looking at the ceiling. "Maybe I ought to go see Acey Jennings's son, what's his name, Porter, about going to work for him. You still got that address Acey give you? Maybe I ought to write and see if he still wants me to work there."

Numb, Annie Bee set down the pan of potatoes, wiped her hands, and went to the Bible to find the slip of paper Acey had given her at her mother's funeral. Handing it to him, she asked, "You tired of living here?"

"Well, sure, ain't never been much of a place to live." He was spelling out the address. Then he looked at her. "Ain't that why we came here, so's we could get enough money to buy us a place of our own?"

Not trusting her voice, she gave him the best smile she could muster and nodded earnestly at him, then bent over her potatoes again.

He went on. "I want the younguns to have a place to run and play in the fields and creeks. It cramps a body all up to be cooped up in town. Seems like it was better for you and me too before we come here."

She said nothing, and after a moment, he left the kitchen.

Callie Jane wrote them that Pap was in somewhat better spirits. Warren Spivey had been coming over often and was farming with him on shares. Pap seemed happy to have someone to talk to about crops and things, she said.

Annie Bee remembered her hunch at her mother's funeral and said to Ral, "I wonder if he's sweet on Callie Jane."

Ral frowned. "Ain't he somehow related? Some kind of cousin?"

"No, that's the Hendersons and the Spiveys. And it was your pappy's first wife that was a Spivey, not your ma."

"Reckon that's all right then."

Annie Bee hoped that it would be; she hoped that Callie Jane really loved Warren and wouldn't marry him just for

Pap's sake. But then she reminded herself that the whole thing might just be her imagination.

Annie Bee saw Gavin whenever she could, but she didn't tell him about Acey Jennings until Ral got an answer from Porter asking him to come to Cedar Springs to talk about working. Then she told Gavin only that Ral was going out of town for a couple of days and asked if he could come to spend the night with her.

He agreed, then smiled tight-lipped. "I could be a kind brother-in-law and offer him my car."

She looked down. Since the day he had asked if she would leave Ral, they had not talked about him. Discomfort hung in the air.

Then Gavin said, "Really, now, how is he going to get there?"

"I don't know. Sometimes he can use the coal truck if he pays for the gasoline."

"Well, why don't you tell him I stopped by and you told me he was going and I said he could use the car? It don't make what we're going to do any better to cause him more trouble giving us the chance to do it." Again he smiled, not the warm smile she loved.

Ral's excitement about going to talk with Porter added to the dread Annie Bee felt. All the time she was packing a lunch for him, he talked about the horses Acey had bought and the ones Porter had written him about. She realized as she looked at him that he hadn't been this interested in anything since they had left Stone's Creek.

The dread lasted all day. She tried to drive it away with plans for the dinner. Spring frying chickens weren't old enough to be sold yet, so she bought a hen for roasting, and she walked out past Aunt Polly's to a farm where she had bought strawberries earlier. It was late in the season now, but she thought there might still be some; the last berries, though small, were always especially sweet from the hotter sun. And there were some, and she bought a quart, although she paid a shameful price for them.

But the dread still tinged her eagerness as she cooked supper and fed the children. She herself didn't eat but waited until she had put the children to bed and Gavin had come with the darkness. Then they sat over the food like a couple of newlyweds alone for the first time, not knowing what to say.

She thought of all the other times that they had eaten together, at her parents' table and the Hendersons', in Stone's Creek and in Old Hickory at both his and Mary's and hers and Ral's. She wondered how many hours they had spent together eating. Then she started giggling at her notions and choked on her food.

He looked up and grinned, puzzled, while she tried to control herself.

Finally she regained enough composure to talk. "I'm sorry. I was just wondering why sleeping together's so important; it's eating together that takes so much time."

He shook his head in mock despair. "I should have known better than to fall in love with a child. Now I don't know whether you're saying you'd rather spend all night sitting here eating cold chicken with me, or you want to go straight to bed with a hungry man."

"What I really want is to spend all my time, eating and sleeping, with you."

He smiled his old smile then. "You'd get pretty tired of that soon enough, I reckon. But that's what we can have tonight at least—just being together like old married folks."

"That's what I want too."

They talked as they finished of what each had been doing, but when they were washing the dishes, Gavin said, "All right, now, I've done my duty keeping you from choking to death and helping you clean up the kitchen. It's time you told me what's really on your mind. Does it have anything to do with Ral's trip?''

She heard the anxiety under his words and realized that he must have been worrying since she had first mentioned it. "Yes. He's gone to see Acey Jennings's son about working for him at a place called Cedar Springs.''

He was quiet for a minute. "Well, I had imagined some worse things, like him going to find a lawyer or a pistol. But I'm not sure they would be worse. At least that would mean things were out in the open and I had a chance of keeping you. Now I don't know if I do or not.''

She said nothing for a minute but leaned the chicken platter against the side of the scalding pan so carefully that it barely clicked. "I don't know either.''

They didn't say anything else until they had finished the dishes and moved into the sitting room. She lit the lamp and sat in her usual chair; he was already in his, but he had moved it closer to hers than usual.

"Aren't you going to sew?'' he asked.

"I thought tonight I'd just sit and look at you while we talk.''

"I love to sit and watch you sew. Do you know you get more done than anybody else I know?''

Obediently she got out her mending. "I get that from my mammy, I reckon. She never could sit with her hands empty.''

"Yes. I recollect that about her too. My ma was always sort of sickly.''

"Like Mary.''

"Yes. Reckon I'm not very lucky in my womenfolk. Till you. But I was ma's thirteenth child.''

"It wasn't your fault.''

"No, I meant being unlucky. But I did use to think it was my fault her being wore out and weak all the time.''

He was looking into the distance, and Annie Bee saw for a moment the child he had been, although something about his mouth showed more than childish woe. Strange how a face she knew so well suddenly looked different. Then he looked grown-up again, and she realized that all these days, months, years, she had not been seeing him as he really was, that when she pictured him in her mind, even when she looked at him ordinarily, she saw him as she had seen him long ago, perhaps as her brother Cleavus's gangly teen-age brother-in-law. Now as she really looked, she saw the furrows in his forehead and the gray in the dark rings at his temples.

She pushed her thimble off into her lap and reached across to cup his cheek in her hand.

"What are you doing?" He caught her hand and squeezed it.

"Loving you."

Her thimble fell and rolled in an arc across the floorboards as they stood up, but neither regarded it.

Later as he lay drawing his fingertip down her cheek, he said, "Annie, dear, it really doesn't make much difference whether Ral decides to move to Cedar Springs or not. We can't go on this way even if we both live here for the rest of our lives. I can't go on stealing what belongs to another man. I want you to belong to me. I want us to have our own children if you're willing and to be together all the time without hiding."

"I know, I know. I want to give you children and to be with you all the time." She closed her eyes. "But I can't face telling Ral just yet. Give me till the end of the month. I'll decide by then, whether he wants to move or not." Her arms, independent of her indecision, circled his ribs and clung fast.

The emptiness of the bed roused her from sleep; he was dressing in the gray light before sunrise. His back was toward her. She sat up and watched him wordlessly until he turned to see whether she was awake.

Then she raised her arms and said, ''Good-bye, my dearest.''

They kissed gravely, and he left.

She closed her eyes to the early light of the May day and listened to the birds calling their same notes over and over as they must have been doing since Eden.

III. Divisions

Even before he spoke, Ral's face when he got back told her that he at least had decided what he wanted. "Annie Bee, you'll love it! Porter has fourteen mares and two fine stallions, and the land there's just right for horses—it's got bluegrass growing out of limestone and red rock, just like in Kentucky, to make the horses' bones strong. And land's not costly; we've already got enough to get us a pretty good place. We can have a place of our own!"

Annie Bee responded as enthusiastically as she could, but he scarcely noticed. By then he was looking for the children to tell them about the wonderful new home they would have.

Over dinner he told her that Porter had a little house on his farm that they could live in while they picked out a farm and built a house if need be. "There's two or three places already for sale around close; folks up there's moving down here to get work." He shook his head in wonder at their stupidity.

Porter was offering him pretty good wages—higher than Acey and Gwaltney had paid. And they would have the crops and stock from their own farm to earn on. "Of course, we'll have to be pretty close for a while till we can stock the place. Sure would be nice if we could get some horses of our own." He looked off into the future.

Annie Bee thought of Maude and the resorption. But she kept his plate filled and responded when it was expected.

That night he made love to her. As the hair of his chest brushed the skin of her breasts, he seemed like a wolf over her. She felt something in him to fear.

Leathie wrote that she was coming to visit, and Annie Bee realized how much she longed to see her friend from home. They had not been together since Annie Bee had driven back to Stone's Creek with Gavin for her mother's funeral, and now that seemed like a lifetime ago. Even if she couldn't tell Leathie about Gavin, it would be a comfort just to see her again.

But when Annie Bee and Ral met Leathie at the steamboat landing, her face promised little comfort. She looked tired, of course, but she also wore a sort of stubborn despair. And she was angry.

After his initial outpouring about Cedar Springs, even Ral saw that something was wrong and began asking about family.

When he got to Nate, she turned her head and looked out the truck window. "I wouldn't know. I ain't seen him in more'n a month. He's more like to be down here somewhere than he is to be home. More like to be anywhere than with me."

"Why? What's wrong with you and Nate?"

"Ain't Annie Bee told you?" She looked at Annie Bee. "I'm not holding it again you, of course, Annie Bee, but he's always throwing you up to me talking about how you've gotten citified and how I'm nothing but a country hick. He's part right, at least; you do look pretty all fancied up like city women."

The women each held a child on her lap. Annie Bee looked down at Clara's red-gold head to escape Leathie's clear eyes; she felt as if Leathie could see the changes inside her as well as out. "Thank you, but you look pretty yourself."

Ral said, "You've not answered my question, Sis. Has something happened between you and Nate? I know he's not settled down since he got back from the war; he's always had a itchy foot. But he just wants you to pretty up some yourself so he can show you off more."

"He wants more than that. First he wanted me to leave home and go traipsing off after him all over the world. And now he don't want me at all." She turned her face away again, but her voice was bitter.

"Now, Leathie, you've just got hurt and took his words wrong somehow. You and Nate's been together long as me and Annie Bee."

"Humph! There's not much way I could mistake his words; he asked me to divorce him. Ask Annie Bee; he told her he wanted a divorce when he come down here at your birthday-time."

Ral looked away from the road toward his wife. "Is that true? He said that to you back then?"

"Yes," she answered, looking ahead.

He said nothing.

Leathie said, "He's not changed his mind. But I'm not going to change mine neither."

Leathie settled into the children's bedroom, and they talked about safe family things through early dinner. Ral had taken a half-day off to meet Leathie at the dock but had to go to work that afternoon. Clara and Nathan claimed their aunt's attention until their mother made them take a nap. Then she settled down with Leathie over coffee.

Leathie told her that everyone was saying that Callie Jane would marry Warren Spivey.

"Is he a good man?" Annie Bee asked.

"Far as anybody can tell. I don't know whether a body can."

Annie Bee took a slow drink and debated opening the subject that was in both their minds. "Do you want to talk about Nate now, Leathie?"

"I don't know that there's a lot to talk about. He says he told you when he was here before that he wanted a divorce so he could marry this nurse in Nashville. He don't say you approved." Her look questioned Annie Bee.

"Of course I didn't approve! Oh, Leathie, I'm so sorry for you. For you both. I can't think he don't—doesn't love you anymore."

"Well, if he does, he sure don't show it. He told me he'd done give me grounds to divorce him, and he'd do or say anything he could to be free. I told him I wouldn't divorce him even if he brought his woman into our house and slept with her right there in front of me. He said then that there was more grounds for divorce than adultery, and that if he got work somewhere else and I wouldn't follow him there, he could divorce me. It don't seem fair, but I went and asked Squire Gwaltney, and he told me it was so, that a wife's got to follow her husband wherever he goes. Nate left home to find work in Nashville, and I come down here to find him. I figured he'd've come to see you all and I could find him that way. But I reckon he outsmarted me and didn't let you know neither."

"No, we ain't—we've not heard from him since he was here in April."

"Well, I reckon I'll have to find him some other way then."

"Leathie, are you sure you want him? He's my brother, and I don't approve of what he's done, but maybe you'd be better off without him since—"

Leathie finished what she couldn't. "Since he don't care about me no more nohow. Why, Annie Bee, I'm surprised you'd think such a thing. Divorce is sin. Even if we didn't care nothing about each other now, it would be wrong to get a divorce."

"Molly Lou's divorced." She watched Leathie's face to catch the surprise, but it didn't come.

"I know; she told me. But she didn't tell me to make me let Nate go; she told me so's I'd keep him."

"I don't see how it could show that."

"Well . . . it's Molly Lou's story, but I reckon she wouldn't mind me telling you, since you're Ral's wife and almost a sister. And somebody's done told you some of it, I reckon."

"Yes, Mary told me." Annie Bee remembered Mary's wishing that Gavin would marry Molly Lou after Mary died.

"Well, then, you knew sooner than anybody told me. Anyhow, after Nate asked me to go to law against him, I was telling her, and she said no, I shouldn't, that we might want each other again and it would be too late.

"I asked her what she meant, and she said it had been that way for her. Seems she was going out with Squire Gwaltney before Mr. Elliott started courting her, and they was in love with each other, but his ma didn't want him to marry and leave her, his paw being new dead and all them little sisters to see to. Anyhow, he and Molly Lou done what they shouldn't ought to till they was married, and somehow it turned her again him. And that's when Mr. Elliott come courting, and she run off with him to get rid of the squire.

"But he followed after her to Ridgefield, Mr. Elliott or not, and she knowed then that she loved him and left Mr. Elliott, but she wouldn't marry the squire because it would be more sin. She wouldn't even ride with him; walked home the whole way, him driving the buggy beside her, right up to our wagon road, him begging her all the way. But it was done too late then since she'd done married Mr. Elliott."

"But Mary told me Mr. Elliott divorced her later. Wouldn't the squire take her then?"

"I reckon men'll do whatever they want to get what they

want. But she wouldn't take him; divorce or no divorce, it would be nothing but adultery. And she said I shouldn't let Nate go neither; he might want loose now, but later he might not, and it would be too late for both of us.''

Annie Bee remembered hearing the same judgment before from Mary. Now it was a judgment on her as well as her brother, but she still meant what she told Leathie: ''Well, I'll help you all I can, and I hope it all turns out all right.'' She didn't promise to pray about it; that would have seemed presumptuous of her.

Leathie thanked her, then excused herself to nurse a headache.

Annie Bee thought after Leathie left the room to lie down that her friend seemed to have built a wall around herself; it protected, but it cut her off from them too.

Well, at least her troubles kept her from looking too closely at Ral and Annie Bee.

She wondered if she should give Leathie Amy Kay Tucker's name. Finding her would most likely be the fastest way of finding Nate.

That night when they were undressing for bed, Ral asked Annie Bee, ''You talk with Leathie today about Nate?''

She told him that she had and outlined what Leathie had said about following Nate to keep him from getting a divorce.

''Well, they'd have to serve papers on her before he could divorce her nohow, and then if she didn't want to give him grounds, she could go wherever he is and he wouldn't have no more grounds. But it don't seem right to be so set on keeping him whether he wants to or not; she can't force the law to make him want her.'' He dropped one shoe and began unlacing the other.

''I don't know what the right of it is now.''

''Well, there can't be no right to it no more. From what you said, he's already had this Nashville woman, and even if he goes back to Leathie, they're neither one like to be happy with the other'n. Leathie's my sister, and I love her, but she's not done enough outright wrong herself to be forgiving to others. I've knowed Nate since he was fourteen, and he's as good a friend as a man could have. But he's not what you call steady, either. He'd always have his fun now and put off paying till later."

She was already in bed. "What can they do, then?"

"I don't know. They'll have to work it out for themselves." He snuffed out the light and climbed into bed. "That's not my problem."

She didn't ask what his problem was.

The next day Annie Bee told Leathie what Ral had said about Nate having to serve papers on Leathie and her being able to find him that way. She didn't tell her Amy Kay's name or that she worked at Vanderbilt Hospital. She told herself that it wouldn't do Leathie any good to know and that it would be a betrayal of her brother, but she felt like a deceiver with him against her friend.

Leathie talked with Ral about the situation that night and decided to go back home in a few days.

While she stayed, Annie Bee took some time off from her patients to show Leathie a little of the city. Annie Bee thought it might be her own last chance to see some of the sights before Ral buried her on some rocky horse farm in Cedar Springs.

They went in with Ral one morning, and the women and children rode the streetcar from downtown to the zoo at Glendale Park, the end of the streetcar line. It was the first time that Annie Bee as well as Leathie had ridden on the electric cars, and it cost a nickel apiece. But Annie Bee had decided to enjoy the day regardless of the expense. She even bought peanuts and popcorn from the vendors there, although they had brought a picnic lunch.

There was a mineral spring outside the gate to the park, and Leathie drank the water there despite the taste; she said her mother had said that mineral water purified the blood.

But Annie Bee bought them all some bottled sarsaparilla, saying that was good for the blood too and smelled and tasted a whole lot better.

Annie Bee and Leathie discussed but rejected the roller coaster, but the children loved the merry-go-round; indeed, they were induced to leave it only by the lure of the animal cages.

The women thought that it was ridiculous that some of the city people there had to go to a zoo to see their first buzzard. Many of the other animals were quite ordinary too: rabbits, turtles, goats, ducks, and sheep. But the monkeys, bison, bears, pelican, and alligator were novelties. Peafowl walked everywhere; sometimes the cocks spread their gorgeous tails. Leathie loved the colorful parrots and cockatiels in the aviary too, but Annie Bee watched the other birds there fly up to the wire-mesh roof and seek a way out. They made her sad.

They ate their lunch in a pavilion with many other picnickers. The children were tired by then, so Annie Bee spread out the tablecloth that she had brought on the ground under a tree so they could take a nap. She and Leathie were talking about the many things to do in the park. "I'll have to tell Prue about this; she should bring her children here sometime."

"Is she the woman that keeps Clara and Nate?"

"Yes." Annie Bee debated. "She's divorced, you know."

"There you go, throwing it up to me again. I swear, Annie Bee, sometimes I think you want me and Nate to get divorced. I don't know how you can approve of such. I wouldn't let a woman like that keep my children."

Annie Bee thought, *Or a woman like me either, if you just knew.* But she said nothing.

Leathie's departure was unhappy in a different way from the unhappiness of the visit. When she started to leave them and board the boat, she cried. All at once the wall she had put around herself seemed to fall down, and she was the old Leathie, sweet and open, but hurt.

Going home, Annie Bee and Ral didn't say anything for a while. Then Annie Bee asked, "Do you think they'll ever work it out?"

Ral said, "I don't know. He's your brother. And you seem to know a lot more about him than I do."

After Annie Bee finished her next weekly report to Dr. Baker, he told her, "You're the best nurse I've ever had. How old are you?"

"Twenty-two, sir."

"You know more now about nursing than many nurses twice your age. You ought to get nurse's training. The Catholic hospital's less costly than Vanderbilt, and the sisters have a good program. A bright young woman like you could go through it in two or three years even if you had to do work at home. There's a new Protestant hospital being built in Nashville, but it will be a while before it will be ready to accept student nurses."

"I don't know—I don't think I could get away from my family to learn."

"Well, think about it. If you decide to, I could lend you some money and you could pay me back later out of what you earned. I could use you at the office or making rounds either.

Perhaps there would even be a hospital here in Old Hickory by then.''

"Thank you, sir, but I'll have to think about it.'' She thought as she spoke that it would never be possible, but she was glad that he had suggested it.

IV. A Wedding

A letter from Callie Jane announced that she and Warren Spivey were to be married. The letter talked more about Pap's happiness than about Callie Jane's, and Annie Bee hoped that her sister was not marrying just to please their father.

Ral was willing to go to Stone's Creek for the wedding, and Gavin offered them the use of his car. The wedding was to be on a Saturday, so Ral and Annie Bee arranged to take off the Friday before from their jobs.

Nate came by one day and told her that he planned to go too, and Annie Bee wondered what would happen when he and Leathie saw each other.

The drive to Stone's Creek kept reminding her of that other drive in the same car. But that had been with Gavin. Ral was a good driver after all his months of working for the coal company, and they seemed to have fewer flat tires, although there were a good many. And the May weather bore little resemblance to the February cold of the funeral trip. But they didn't talk much, and Ral didn't join in the games that Annie Bee tried to entertain the children with. She kept thinking of Gavin and wondering what it would be like to have him beside her instead of Ral.

The first sight of Callie Jane dispelled Annie Bee's doubts. Her baby sister, by now three years older than Annie Bee had been when she had married, glowed with joy. The mention of Warren's name was enough to send the blood into her face.

And Pap too did seem happy, almost as he had been before Mammy had died. After he had given her a bear hug, he put his arm around Ral and said, "Well, boy, I'm going to get another son. A man can't have too many, or girls either. I'm glad you've brought my girl back so I get to see her and the grandbabies some." He turned his attention to Clara and Nathan then.

Clara was excited about the wedding, the first she remembered, and she wanted to see Aunt Callie Jane's dress more than to play with Grandpap.

Nathan was a better companion for his grandfather, who carried the boy on his shoulders everywhere they went.

Nate arrived just before supper; Leathie wasn't with him, and Pap asked whether she was sick.

Nate said, "No, sir, she's just got some things to do and isn't coming over till tomorrow."

Callie Jane's worried look told Annie Bee that she knew about their brother's trouble, but Pap didn't. Annie Bee asked, "Is Warren coming tonight?"

Callie Jane seemed relieved at the change of subject. "Yes, he's going to eat with his folks, but then he'll come over to see you all."

"I don't reckon he cares about seeing you none," Nate said.

Callie Jane blushed again. "Reckon we'll see enough of each other soon enough."

Nate laughed. "Well, I warrant you'll see *more* of each other than you've seen before. Less you've been eating dinner before you've had grace said."

Callie Jane's face was red enough to light a fire by.

Annie Bee took pity and said, "Speaking of grace, it's time to sit down and start supper."

While they were still passing the bowls, Nate said, "Callie Jane, are you sure you want to get hitched up to this Spivey boy?"

"Of course, Nate. I wouldn't marry him less I was sure. Why, you know, I've known him all my life, and there's nobody else I've ever really wanted to marry."

"Well, I know it's none of my business, but you're my baby sister, and I just don't want you to get hurt."

Ral said, "That's how I feel about my sisters too. Don't reckon there's much a body can do to keep them safe though." His look toward Nate was accusing.

Nate didn't answer. Annie Bee and Callie Jane looked at their food. Fortunately, Clara had remembered her old hold over Pap by then, and her chatter filled the silence until talk began on prices and weather.

When Warren came over, he spent quite a generous time talking with them all before he asked Callie Jane if she wanted to go out on the porch to sit in the swing awhile. Callie Jane asked if anyone else wanted to come, but everyone emphatically denied any interest at all in enjoying the soft May evening.

Annie Bee's disclaimer was sincere: she was quite tired enough from the trip to look forward to going to bed, and she soon had the children tucked into a pallet beside her and Ral's bed in Nate's old room; he would sleep in the front room on a pallet that night. Ral stayed up talking with Pap for a while; the last thing she heard before drifting off was a discussion of Squire Gwaltney's horses.

Cleavus and the older sisters arrived Saturday morning, each bringing their families and enough food for threshers, as Annie Bee had. And of course Callie Jane had been cooking for a week. The wedding would be in the late afternoon, and they would have the wedding dinner right after it.

While Sally, Wilda, and Idell put lunch on the table, Annie Bee helped Callie Jane arrange her hair. She thought of how much Mammy would have enjoyed seeing her lovely red-haired daughter and hoped that she herself would see Clara married someday. Then she and Callie Jane took the flowers Callie Jane had cut Friday and arranged them and placed them through the house and on the porch.

At lunch Cleavus's wife Sally asked about her brother Gavin.

Annie Bee said nothing, but let Ral answer. "Well, I saw him yesterday when I went to get the car. He's all right. But we've not seen him to amount to much for a good spell now. Reckon he's pretty busy with the building going on for the new rayon plant."

"You going to work for them now, Ral?" Cleavus asked.

"Well, I don't know. There's two or three things I could do; I ain't rightly decided yet."

"I hear they're going to pay good money."

"Yeah, but money don't make everything. A man's life's gone soon enough without spending it shut up in some box doing what everybody else tells him to."

Pap joined in. "Well, that's right enough. I spent my life out in the sun and rain and wouldn't have it no other way."

"That's what I like best too," Ral said. "Yessir."

The Henderson sisters, Leathie, Molly Lou, and Lusetta, and Hoyt and Trubie and their children came for the wedding, of course. Annie Bee took the newest child, Jane, to hold but gave her back to Trubie as soon as she realized that the baby was wet through. Most of the other neighbors came too. Mr. Henderson had stayed at home. He never went out anymore, Leathie said, and they were a little anxious about leaving him alone. But Warren's uncle Walter Spivey, the old singer blind from his birth, had offered to stay with Mr. Henderson.

"Much good he could do!" Nate offered. "Talk about the blind helping the crazy!"

Annie Bee was appalled at Nate's talking about Leathie's father that way with her right there. And of course Warren heard what Nate said about Warren's uncle too. But she was glad that Nate was staying beside Leathie like a dutiful husband; there was no call to publish to the whole county that they weren't getting along.

Callie Jane looked beautiful. Her dress was a blue so pale that it was almost white, made with tucks all down the bodice. At her waist she wore a little perfume flask Warren had given her, a crystal teardrop about two inches long with a silver top set with tiny sapphires through which was threaded a deep blue satin ribbon. Her eyes shone like the sapphires. In his store-bought suit Warren made Annie Bee think of the pictures she had seen of Douglas Fairbanks or some such movie star.

The preacher married them on the front porch so everyone could see. Annie Bee stood up with Callie Jane, and Warren's brother Ervin stood up with him. Then the wedding party and all the guests went through the house and filled their plates at the table and spread picnic cloths on the lawn to eat from.

As soon as everyone had finished and the food was cleared away, the families that had to travel some distance to reach home that night packed up and left. Of course Trubie led Hoyt away too before the dishes were washed. Callie Jane had told the women that she didn't want them to bed the bride. But no one assumed that she wanted them to stay late either. So all the neighbors except for Ral's family left soon too, and Annie Bee and Ral put their things in Gavin's car to go to the Hendersons, where they were to spend the night.

They told the newlyweds and Pap good-bye and walked down to the car. There wasn't room for everybody to ride, so Annie Bee suggested that Molly Lou go with Ral while she and the children walked with the other Hendersons.

Molly Lou was of course insulted. "I may be old, Annie Bee, but I'm not decrepit yet. I can walk as far as you, I warrant."

"I'm sure you can, Molly Lou, and if you want to, I'll be glad to have your company. But I want to walk over the fields the way we used to, and I thought you might want to talk with your brother awhile."

Molly Lou said, "Maybe Nate would rather ride with him."

Nate had been helping Ral crank up the car. He wiped his hands without answering, and Annie Bee expected him to make some excuse for not going to the Hendersons'. But he said, "No. I thought I'd walk with my wife and the other womenfolk."

And he did, so Molly Lou rode with Ral. The walk was pleasant, with the lightning bugs just coming out and the children running after them and Lusetta running after the children, still half a child herself. Annie Bee and Leathie talked about things they used to do as children, and Nate was quiet except for answers to Annie Bee's remarks to him; Leathie didn't talk to him nor he to her.

Annie Bee was shocked at Mr. Henderson's appearance. He was as thin as an old tree-limb with knobby joints, and his eyes were sunken so far under his brows that they showed only in the reflection of the lamp's flame. She didn't think he knew who she and Ral were, and even the children roused no response from him.

Ral drove Walter Spivey home, loaded with thanks and two platefuls from the dinner: one of meat and vegetables, the other of cake and pie. Mr. Henderson ate what they had brought for him, and then he went to bed right away. Annie Bee put the children to bed too; she would sleep with them on pallets in the big workroom with Molly Lou and Lusetta that night, and Ral would sleep up in the loft.

She wondered where Nate would sleep, upstairs with Ral or in the little room with Leathie.

Everyone else was tired but not ready to retire. The women changed from their good dresses into nightgowns, then came back to the lamplit table where Nate was sitting just as they heard Ral's steps on the porch. Annie Bee sat down on one side of Nate, but Leathie sat across the table and left the chair on his other side empty. When Ral came in, he took it after a hesitation.

Lusetta changed from a child into a young lady. "Wasn't the wedding just the prettiest thing? When I get married, I want a wedding just like it."

"Better no weddings at all." Molly Lou was attacking her eternal knitting.

Nate responded. "Maybe they're not so bad after all."

Everyone looked at him. Molly Lou had even stopped in mid-row.

"I mean, hearing what I heard today made me think again about what people promise when they get married. I reckon I need to live up to what I promised. I know I've not been a very good husband. And I ought to try to do what I said I would."

Annie Bee reached over to squeeze his arm, but it wasn't her place to say anything.

And Leathie didn't either. She sat with tears rolling down her face.

Nate looked at her. "Leathie, I won't make no more promises. But I'll try to live up to the ones I made when we married if you want me to."

"Why, Nate? Just because you said them?"

"Well, yes, because I said them, promised, and a man ought to keep his promises, 'specially to a woman."

"Is that what you want? Am I what you want?"

"Now, Leathie, don't ask me that. I'll do the best I can to be a good husband to you."

She had quit crying, and her voice was calm. "No. You don't want me, and I won't hold you. I can live without you, if that's what you want, better than I can live with you. I don't want your duty. If you don't want me, I don't want you."

Nate wasn't jubilant. "Do you really mean that?"

"Yes. I do." And she smiled.

Nobody said anything for a long minute.

Nate bent his head, then said, "Well—reckon I'll go over to Joe Conyer's tonight then. I'll come back tomorrow and we'll talk about . . . things." He stood up and rubbed his hands together and looked at her, then at the rest.

Most of them weren't looking at him.

Then he left.

Leathie went into her room, the room she and Nate had shared, and closed the door. The rest all went to bed without so much as a "Good night."

Except for the children and Lusetta, breakfast the next morning was quiet. Everyone seemed to be wrapped in his own thoughts. Leathie's eyes were red.

Molly Lou too seemed especially agitated; she put pepper on the eggs twice and forgot the salt, and she almost burned the biscuits.

It was Ral who brought up the question in everyone's mind. "Leathie, do you really mean you don't want Nate no more?"

She looked at him straight. "Yes. I don't want him if he don't want me."

"You know he'll go and marry that nurse then."

214

"That's all right too."

"But it's a sin."

"I don't reckon it's a sin more'n what's gone on already. And what might go on if I don't let him go."

"You two ain't had much of a marriage. I mean, he left for the war right after you all got married, and since he got back, I don't reckon . . . I mean, you probably . . ."

"We ain't had much time together since we got married, but we had years and years to get to know each other. Same as you and Annie Bee. We know each other pretty well."

Ral didn't look at either one of them.

It was Molly Lou who began crying then. Leathie rose and went to her. "Don't cry for me. I'm all right. I'm not going to pine away and die."

"No. You're not. But there's things worse. You'll be like me, alone, with nobody to care for you, getting old and mean."

"You don't have to be alone. Haskell Gwaltney loves you."

Molly Lou's response was deep sobs that shook her whole body. "We can't ever have each other. We'll both die lone."

"Why should you, Molly Lou? You're married to him more than you was ever married to Mr. Elliott, body and heart."

"But it's wrong."

"And is this right, for you two to spend your lives not two miles from each other, loving each other and not ever giving your love to each other? Mr. Elliott don't profit from your misery."

Molly Lou only shook her head and sobbed.

Ral and Annie Bee packed their things in the car, said their good-byes, and left as soon as they could. Annie Bee's mind was in turmoil. She and Ral didn't talk much on the drive home either.

V. Preparations

The visit to Stone's Creek for the wedding and catching up on her work afterward kept Annie Bee from seeing Gavin for over a week. When she did go to him again, she was conscious of the deadline that she had imposed upon herself. It was past the end of the month, and she had not decided whether to break with Ral or not.

The day was beautiful: more like spring than summer, with a breeze that suggested the cool nights they had been having. She and Gavin made love, and then she told him about the visit, including the strange revelations that Nate, Leathie, and Molly Lou had made. He didn't say anything about Leathie's change of heart but squeezed her hand hard.

She talked him into driving to the hill past Aunt Polly's, although he was apprehensive about their being seen together. She wanted to show him her hillside. She wore a motoring veil over her hat so that no one would recognize her if they were noticed.

He pulled the car over to the side of the road, and they walked up the hill to the outcroppings of rock in the edge of the woods. The trees were heavy with summer; their shade was dark.

The leaves and underbrush made it a private-enough place to sit and talk, but for a while he just looked out over the countryside. She leaned back against a tree and studied the straight line of his nose and the rounded lines of his mouth and chin.

Finally he looked at her. "A man kind of forgets how beautiful it can be out here away from the smoke and mud. Makes me remember why Ral wants to get out in the country again. What do you want, Annie?"

"I don't know. At least, I know I can't have what I want because I want everything. I want the town and this. And I want you all the time, but I don't want to hurt Ral." She paused. "I've been thinking about what he'll do if I tell him. He'll crawl into a hole like a groundhog and not come out at all unless he wants to fight somebody."

"And what'll happen if you don't tell him?"

"Well . . . I don't know what'll happen to you. I don't like to think about that. If you find somebody else, I won't want to think about you with her. And if you don't, it'll hurt me to think about you lone. And sometimes I think I'll lose you anyhow. Someday you'll look at me and know I'm not good enough for you."

He pulled her close and kissed her. "My dearest girl, no one's good enough to be loved. That's why we can love each other." He laughed at his own strange logic. "But what about you? What'll happen to you if you go on with Ral the rest of your life?" He drew back and looked at her almost sternly.

"I don't know. Sometimes I think I'll just shrivel up inside, like a rotten apple left lying on the ground. Ral . . . well, Ral's like his pappy. And Mr. Henderson always somehow scared me."

"Are you scared Ral will hurt you?"

She thought about it a moment. But she shook her head. "No . . . that's not what I meant even about his pappy. He's like all twisted in on himself. Now Ral's mammy wasn't like that. But the two of them . . . they were strange together. It's like they never talked to each other or even touched each other, like they were strangers to each other all their lives, all the time they were married to each other. Each one was locked up in a separate world. And look at their children— none of them what you'd call happy either."

"Hoyt seems right happy. And Mary—I like to think she was happy. But I know what you mean. If I didn't think I could give you more than Ral, I wouldn't ask you."

"Oh, Gavin, the one thing I *am* sure about is that you've already given me more than Ral ever could. But that makes me sorry for him too; I keep thinking he'll be like Molly Lou, lone and bitter against the world, or like his old half brother Clem, who's crawled back in his hollow and lies there like an old wounded bear. Nora's not what you'd call wounded, but she's lone and—and covered, like with a husk. Or maybe Ral would be like Leathie if she and Nate get divorced."

"Well, Annie dear, you'll have to be the one to decide. I thought once I'd choose for you and just go away and leave you alone. But I can't do that anymore. I want you if you'll have me. And I won't go away unless you tell me to." He looked at her so steadily that she felt as if she could see everything in his mind, and the strength and love she found there warmed her like the sun dappling his face through the leaves.

Nate was waiting when she came back home from her nursing a few days later. After the children had grown tired of him, he told her that he and Leathie had decided to get a divorce. He looked happy, but she noticed that there were lines in his forehead and at the corners of his mouth.

"How do you feel about it?"

"Well, I reckon it's what I've wanted. Annie Bee, you have to meet Amy Kay too to know how I feel. But Leathie—well, she's a fine woman too. Ain't many like her." He ran his hand back through his hair.

"No. Not many loves a man enough to let him go." She wondered which of her men she would have to let go. Would it be whichever one she loved the most?

"But I know Amy Kay loves me too. And I want her. Not being with her. . . . Well, when I'm not with her, it's like I ain't got a part of me. Maybe that rib God took out of old Adam." He grinned, but she knew he meant it. "I'd like for you to meet her."

"I'd like that too. But Ral. . . . I don't know if he'll feel that way."

"No. No, reckon he might not. I'll study on it and see what we can do."

The next day Nate stopped again and asked if she could take off Friday and go with Amy Kay to visit a sick aunt in Gallatin; they could ride on the interurban and see a little of the countryside too. She agreed.

That night she told Ral.

He said, "Well, I reckon he'll still be your brother when he's stopped being my sister's husband. But I don't care to meet the whore he's going to replace her with."

She nodded, and they said nothing else about it.

She decided to take the children to Gallatin rather than leave them with Prue; in addition to the savings, she wanted the children with her as a distraction, something to talk about if things were strained.

But the meeting was not as strained as she had expected. Amy Kay didn't look like a loose woman; indeed, she looked a lot like Leathie, small and neat, not someone a body would notice in a crowd. Her brown hair was short—bobbed, they called it—like that of some of the fashionable women in the newspapers. But she had a sweet smile, almost shy. She didn't say much when Nate introduced them. And she looked as anxious as Annie Bee felt.

The interurban was like the streetcars, run by electricity. Nate insisted on paying for all of them, so she didn't know how much it cost. But he didn't go with them; he took them to the sheds at the beginning of the line and waved them away.

At first the women talked about the children. Amy Kay praised Clara's red hair and her and Nathan's eyes, dark brown like Ral's.

Annie Bee asked, "Do you want children?"

"Yes. That is, if Nate does."

Annie Bee wondered if Amy Kay's nurses' training had told her about any better ways not to have children than Mary had known. But she didn't feel comfortable asking that, not yet, and certainly not on the interurban. She did ask what Amy Kay's job was like, and Amy Kay started telling and asking about Annie Bee's, and soon they were talking about patients and treatments. Annie Bee thought how much she would like to have someone close by to talk with like that all the time.

Gallatin seemed like a sleepy village compared to the city. But Annie Bee knew that it was bigger than Ridgefield, much less Stone's Creek. She wondered what Cedar Springs was like; Ral's report had been only about its farmland.

Amy Kay's aunt was not a very old woman, nor did she seem really ill; her husband had died, and she seemed to have turned to invalidism as a way to fill her time. The younger women mostly just listened to her list of complaints. But she had prepared them a good lunch, creamed chicken on cornbread, and she was understanding of the children, who napped after eating.

On the return trip, Annie Bee felt more at ease with Amy Kay and asked her what she and Nate had planned.

"Well, of course, we'll have to wait to get married until the divorce is final. That'll be a year. He's going to try to find work in Nashville. He's so good with machines; he's going to go out to the airport and see if he can get work.''

"Yes, he told me how much he liked working on the airplanes in France. He's liked fixing things since he was a little boy. I remember one time he took Mammy's Regulator clock apart. She was going to whip him, and he talked her into waiting to see if he could put it together again so it would work. And he did!''

Amy Kay said, ''He's good at that too—talking his way out of trouble!''

They laughed, and Annie Bee started telling about things he had done as a boy, and Amy Kay told about things he had done in France. Then she told about what she had seen of the war there—soldiers who had lost their frozen toes when their socks were pulled off, those who got gangrene, those who "went west," as she called dying.

Annie Bee breathed a prayer of gratitude that Nate had come home whole; saint or sinner, he was her brother.

And she realized that she liked this new sister-in-law-to-be, divorce or not; dear Leathie would always be her childhood friend and sister to her heart. But Amy Kay was worth learning to love.

Ral asked nothing about the trip, and she volunteered nothing.

The next Monday night Porter Jennings stopped to try to persuade Ral to come to Cedar Springs right away. He was buying a new filly and wanted Ral to begin training her. "My pa says you're the best man he knows for breaking a racehorse, and I want this'n to be broke right.''

"Well, that's mighty kind of Acey to say so. But I never liked to talk about breaking them. Seems to me that's what too many people do—they break them so they'll mind, but

222

they break their spirit too. What I like to do with a horse is make her want to do what I want her to do but make her know she's free. If she knows that, she'll run her hardest and do her best." He looked at Annie Bee, who had been watching him while he talked.

But she looked down again at her sewing and told herself that his talk was only about horses.

Ral didn't give Acey an answer but promised to tell him the next day whether he would go to Cedar Springs that week.

After he saw Porter to the door, he came back and sat down across the table from Annie Bee again. "Well, shall we go or not?" he asked her.

She looked up, surprised. "It's not for me to say."

"I reckon you've got something to say about it that you've not been saying. A man don't have to look hard to see that you're not exactly excited about going. Reckon it's time I found out why."

Desperate for something to say, she told Ral then about Dr. Baker's offer to lend her money for nurse's training and hire her as a real nurse.

When she had finished, he said nothing at first but kept looking at her.

She continued to sew.

Finally he asked, his voice quiet and even, "Is that what you want?"

"I don't know. I don't know."

He sat and watched her awhile longer, then got up and went into their bedroom.

He was asleep when she went to bed, and she fell asleep too. But she dreamed that she got a pistol and shot him, and when she awoke, she saw the dark wound at his temple flowing blood again. Then she realized that it was only the dream and the shadow of his black hair across his face in the dim light. But she thought, *I can't tell him. I can't let him know that I don't want him. That would be like killing him sure enough. I'm the one that would kill, not him.*

Then she lay awake thinking of what their life together would be like—never touching each other except in that strange joining called making love that didn't join and wasn't necessarily love, working every day together like wheels of a railroad car, run by an iron rod that held them together and at the same time kept the center of each of them apart from the other. They would live on a farm like the ones they had known, a little rockier or a little richer, but a place where they would gamble on the rain and drought, the sun and hail and prices and the speed of horses for the bread they ate and the things they bought their children. She would catch a few babies and grow old like her mother.

And she would remember.

The next morning she told Ral that she thought he should accept Porter's offer. He smiled like a boy at a church Christmas tree who gets a jackknife he has wanted a long time.

Then he said, "Thank you. I'll try to make it up to you about being a nurse."

She controlled her voice. "Oh, that's all right. It doesn't matter."

"And—about our other troubles here."

She didn't look at him. Whatever pain he had cost her before he got work or when her mother died, her guilt had canceled the debt. His apology cut like a reprimand. "You don't owe me anything," she said. "When'll we leave?"

He told her his plans for leaving the job with the coal company and joining Porter, who had come to Franklin just south of Nashville to look at some stock and would be going back in a day or two. They agreed that she would stay to finish their business in town. Then she would join him.

224

After Ral had left for the city, she went to Gavin's workshop and haltingly told him what she had done. She felt like a child called before the teacher's desk for not knowing her lesson. "I couldn't tell him, Gavin. I couldn't hurt him."

"So you're hurting me."

She saw his hurt in his twisted mouth and furrowed forehead. She wished that he would kiss her; she couldn't remember their last kiss. But she knew that he wouldn't.

She hurried away, looking down so that her sunbonnet would hide her tears.

She went next to Dr. Baker's office, which was at the side of his house. He was gone, but the secretary promised to tell him that she needed to see him. She had left similar messages before when he needed to see a patient, so she knew that he would get in touch with her.

There was not a lot of other business to do: she would have to see their landlord and tell Prue, who already knew they might leave. She put those tasks off till Wednesday. She would have a hard time seeing Leona, who never left her housekeeping job before dark except on Thursday, when Annie Bee would have to be packing; Annie Bee wouldn't go out after dark with Ral gone. She wrote a note to Leona and another to Aunt Polly and mailed them. She wasn't sure that either one could read, but maybe they could get someone to read the notes to them.

All day she thought not about the bleakness of her prospects but about the times she had spent with Gavin, the touches and words they had exchanged, and about what their life together could have been like, full with each other.

Dr. Baker stopped in the afternoon. He seemed genuinely regretful that she was leaving, and after he left, she imagined what it would have been like to be a real nurse in a dark blue wool cape taking care of people in a hospital or helping the doctor at his office.

Ral was pleased when he got home that the coal company had paid him the whole week's wages. He had thought they might dock him even for what he had earned that week since he was quitting without notice. "Everthing's working out fine," he said. "It must be that the Lord means for us to go."

She reflected wryly that she was the Presbyterian, but said nothing; after all, she couldn't really expect it to be the Lord's will for her to stay.

After supper she saw him off to talk with Porter, then sat on the porch. The sunset was glorious, turning the summer clouds into rosy mountains. She thought of being always bathed in that light. But although she did not see when it happened, the light died; cloud by cloud, the rose changed to leaden gray.

The heavy scent of Prue's lilies settled over her like funeral flowers. She shivered in the June dusk and went into the house.

VI. Parting

She waited up for Ral to hear their plans. He told her he would go back with Porter the next morning so he could get the little house Porter owned ready for them to move into or maybe even go ahead and buy a place for them. Porter had bought cattle somewhere on the other side of Nashville and would come back Friday to move them. Ral would drive Porter's horse and wagon down that day and load their household things. Then he would help Porter take the cattle back in the truck, and Annie Bee would drive the wagon to Cedar Springs on Saturday.

She got up before dawn on Wednesday to cook breakfast, pack a lunch and a few clothes for Ral, and see him off. They waited on the front porch. It was chill, and she wrapped her shawl tightly around her.

When Porter stopped in his truck, Ral kissed her on the cheek and left. The sun was just coming up.

She stood staring at the empty street a long time, not really seeing it or the familiar house opposite with its muddy yard and grayed wood broken by the blue morning glories gaily climbing strings all along the front porch.

Finally she moved into the house, but each step seemed an effort. Her arms were frozen in the shawl pulled tightly around her. Inside, she went to her bedroom and stood in the doorway, again not seeing. After a while she crawled back into bed and, despite the growing heat of the June day, pulled the covers over her head.

She ignored the children's calls until they found her. Then, delighted that she was playing hide-and-seek with them, they climbed onto the bed and burrowed under the covers with her. She hugged them and tried to make them lie still, but that was impossible, so she got up and dressed and fed them.

But she had no desire to move; all she really wanted to do all that endless day was curl up and lie as still as a stone. She actually did little; she didn't even think, but moved like a sleepwalker. As soon as dark fell, she put the children to bed and went to bed herself. She fell asleep at once.

The next morning she awoke out of a dream of Gavin. He was waiting for her to join him, and then they were going to get in his car and go on a trip, a long trip. It was like the trip they had made to Stone's Creek for her mother's funeral except that the weather was a perfect June day, and she knew that when they left, they would never come back. The car was filled with morning glories. She told Gavin, "They're called Heavenly Blue." She knew that they had been cut off the vines, but they had not shriveled the way morning glories always did. As she and Gavin climbed into the car, the children were with them.

But all at once, as they started, she realized that Nathan was toddling across the road ahead of them. The road was full of snow and ice, and she knew that the car would skid and hit the boy. Then she too was outside the car, running to pull him out of the way. As she did, the car passed them and disappeared in the falling snow.

She awoke thinking, *I can't let him go.* But what she accomplished that day was aimed toward leaving. First she told Prue good-bye. That was hard, although of course Prue already knew from Walter. Both women cried, and they made many promises not to forget each other and to visit every chance they got. But both knew how seldom that was likely to be.

Leaving the children with Prue, she walked to the landlord's to tell him that they would be leaving that week. There was some time left on the rent that they had paid, and she had thought that he might offer to repay part of it, but he didn't, and she didn't ask.

On the way back from his house, she went by the river. She picked her way down the steep bluff path, hanging onto the scrub bushes along the way sometimes. Even the bank was narrow and treacherous. The water was muddy with runoff from some rains that she hadn't seen washing down hills upstream, maybe back home at Stone's Creek even.

She thought how easy it would be to slip into the water and slide down, down, to the rocky bed.

But she knew that she would float. Swim even, despite herself. No, the murky water was no escape.

When she stopped to get the children from Prue, they sat and talked a long time, remembering things that had happened since the Hendersons had moved in. Finally they parted by assuring each other that they didn't have to say good-bye yet, not quite.

She would not say good-bye to Aunt Polly or Leona or Mrs. Thorburn or the Lammingtons or any of the other patients. But she probably would never see any of them again.

That afternoon she began packing in earnest. Her lethargy had lost Wednesday for her. But even now, although she had regained her usual energy, she couldn't seem to get things done. She would come to herself holding some cup or shirt and realize that she had spent long minutes doing nothing, remembering Gavin or just telling herself that she could not leave him, even as she was preparing to.

Then she began imagining what she could do. She could go to him, that very afternoon, take the children and say, "I'm here. I decided. I want you."

And he would take her, and she would send word to Ral and never see him again.

But she couldn't do that. She would have to see him, have to tell him. And his face would close up, and it would be terrible to see that happen to him and terrible to be locked away from him forever.

Maybe she could go to Gavin and have him come back with her to the house as he had the other time Ral had been gone. They would be together that much longer, have that much more before they had nothing.

But that wasn't what she wanted either. It really was sharing the ordinary, the everyday, that mattered more than sleeping together. What made her happy was knowing that he found happiness in being with her. And she knew that he was not happy stealing her from Ral, sneaking around under the cover of darkness. Only her being his wife would bring them what they sought. And she could never be his wife unless she left Ral. So she was back at the place she had started.

She stayed up late that night trying to catch up on the time that she had lost. But she knew as she worked that she was not thinking; again the scent of Prue's lilies seemed to fog her mind. She would pack something and then realize that they would have to use it before they left Saturday. So then she would go to unpack it and not remember where it was.

Finally she gave up and went to bed about midnight, everything in heaps or half-filled boxes or bushel baskets.

Even then she couldn't sleep. She lay thinking of the old

circle: needing Gavin and not wanting to hurt Ral so not being able to tell him so that she could go to Gavin. Near dawn she resigned herself to leaving Gavin. Wasn't that what she had told him she would do? And wasn't it the truth that she couldn't tell Ral? She had had her chance when he had asked why she didn't want to go to Cedar Springs. Now she would never be able to raise the issue again. If only he knew without her having to tell him. If only he knew, and she were free!

Friday was the day Ral was to bring the wagon back to load. Annie Bee arose from her fitful sleep anxious to be packed by the time he arrived.

Her heart felt heavy, like a stone in her ribs. She thought of Gavin with despair: *I'll never see him again.*

Prue came over in midmorning to help pack, but the seven children took their mothers' workday as a holiday. Both women spent more time trying to keep order than packing things, so Prue took the children all home with her to keep while Annie Bee packed in peace. Prue invited Annie Bee to eat at noon, by which time she really had made some progress toward getting ready to leave. But much remained to be done.

Ral arrived earlier than she had hoped, early in the afternoon. He told her that he had found two possible farms to buy but wanted her to see them before he made any commitments. For the moment, they would live in Porter's house.

Then he looked around at the boxes in the front room to plan how to pack the wagon. "This is not all, is it?" He looked at her, puzzled.

"No, there's a lot still to do." She looked down.

"Well, Porter's coming for me in about a hour, and I've got to go with him to get the cattle then. I can load what you've got ready, but it don't look like that's going to be enough."

"I'm sorry. I just didn't get it all done." She felt like a child caught in mischief.

He said nothing else but began loading what was packed. When he had done that, he went next door and talked with Prue, something he usually avoided. Then he came back to the kitchen, where Annie Bee was working.

"I reckon you'd better not come tomorrow. Finish packing, and come when you can. Walter'll help you load the wagon; I talked with his wife about that."

"Gavin can do it."

His smile was thin. "No. He'll be packing your things if you don't come, I reckon. If you come to me, don't ask him to help you."

Her heart jumped. "What do you mean?"

He looked at her gravely. His face was the same she had known for as long as she could remember: oval, with the high forehead, impenetrable eyes, and Indian nose. But everything about him now made her think of a skull, the bare bones sharp and definite under the economical flesh and skin. Everything but the mouth; though fine-drawn, that was generous.

It also seemed somehow defenseless as he spoke: "I'm not asking you to drink the waters of bitterness, like in the Bible. If you want me, then I want you for always. If you don't, you're free to do what you want. But I don't aim to share you with nobody."

She tried to sort out what he was saying. "What do you mean, the waters of bitterness?"

"Don't reckon you've had a call to use that Bible text." He smiled, his lips together. "Well, it's in the fifth chapter of Numbers if you want to look it up. But I'm not asking you to; reckon times is changed since then, and I don't blame you for what's happened no more'n I blame myself. You come to Cedar Springs if you want to. If you don't, leave the mule and wagon and whatever you don't want with Walter, and I'll come back for it."

Her hand was lying on the table. He laid his on top of it for a moment.

232

She did not dare look at his face.

Then he left to go outside and wait for Porter.

So he knew! He knew that she had betrayed him with Gavin. She was sure even before she found the Bible and looked up the passage in Numbers.

Yes, he knew. The waters of bitterness were a test of a woman's fidelity. The jealous husband was to bring her to a priest and offer barley meal without the usual oil and frankincense: an "offering of jealousy, an offering of memorial." Memorial to what? Ah, yes. To bring her iniquity to remembrance. Whose remembrance? Reckon they thought *she* might have forgotten? Women didn't write the Bible, that was sure. Then the priest was to take holy water in an earthen vessel *(all of us are earthen vessels)* and mix it with dust from the floor of the tabernacle *(all dust too)*. Then he was to write curses in a book and wash the curses off with the water and make her drink the water. Sort of like eating her words. Or her vows? And the water would enter into her and cause bitter pain. Then they could go home together and wait for the signs of her guilt: her thigh would rot and her belly swell. Well, that ought to do the job: punishment and preventive for guilty love all in one. She didn't have to read the sentence for the guilty woman; she knew well enough what the law said about that.

She closed the book and went to the front-room window to look at Ral, still waiting outside for Porter. She felt surprised somehow that he stood there looking down the street in the June sunlight, knowing, undestroyed. Then she squeezed the book against her stomach, hard, and ran back into the kitchen.

He knew, and he still touched her hand and said he wanted her and freed her.

Free! Free to go to Gavin! But that was sin. That could not be God's will. She looked at the book and laid it on the kitchen table. Then she sat down and laid her head on her folded arms.

Nothing would come. She had not prayed in so long that

she couldn't begin. But Ral had forgiven her. If he could, surely God could. *Oh, Lord, help me. Let me know Thy will and accept it.*

She stayed there until she felt the quiet around her. Then she returned to the front-room window. The place where Ral had been standing was empty except for the June sunlight. *Oh, Lord, give me a sign.*

She worked hard the rest of the day and the next morning packing; Prue kept the children again. It was almost noon and she was almost through when she brought a load into the front room and saw Gavin standing in the doorway to the porch. Her heart leaped. Perhaps this was her sign: she had not called him, but he had come. He stood there, bringing sunlight into the room.

"Is Ral here?" he asked.

"No. He's gone." She clarified: "Gone ahead to Cedar Springs."

"I reckon you don't want me to see you again, but I saw your wagon and knew you're going. I wanted to tell you not to remember what I said last time."

She set her bundle down. "I can't forget that I hurt you; I never wanted to do that."

"I was hurt, but I was wrong to blame you. You had to hurt me or him, and I've got no rights."

She hesitated, wondering if she should tell him, wondering what he would say. But she had to tell him; he deserved to know too. "Ral knows."

His face twisted. "Did you tell him?"

"No. Reckon he figured it out himself."

He came into the room then and sat heavily on one of the wooden boxes, his head in his hands. He seemed more stricken than Ral had. She watched. So this was her sign.

Finally he raised his eyes. "What did he say?"

234

"He said he didn't blame me. He didn't mean he blamed you, either; said it was as much his fault as mine. He said he still wanted me if I wanted to go; otherwise, he'd send for the mule and what I didn't want."

He looked at her then with wonder. "He let you go. He knows, and he . . ."

She nodded, but gave him time. She knew then, heavy but proud, that he would come to it. She knew him too well not to know that he would come to it faster than she had.

And he did. "So you'll go to him?"

She nodded. "I want you both. But if I went to you, I'd destroy what I love in you. Maybe you'd come to hate me for that. And I'd destroy myself too. And maybe him." She thought of Mr. Henderson, old and lone, looking for Julie. Then she thought of Gavin alone, and she almost lost control. But she went on. "I can't give you what I want to. Better for you to . . . to have someone else."

Pain crossed his face then, and he stood up and turned away. "Maybe you don't want me after all."

Wordless, she crossed to him and put her palms against his back, pressing them over him, his muscles and flesh and bones, so that her hands could remember, then moved around him, feeling his chest, his bare-skinned face.

He embraced her, kissed her, and held her against him. Then he let go of her and left.

The last thing that she packed was her nurse's bag. She took Gavin's letters out of it and put them in her apron pocket, then gathered up the trash to burn, took it out to the burn pile, and set it afire.

She took out the letters and unfolded them. She didn't read them, but passed her hands over the pages. Then she laid them on the blaze. They charred quickly and flew up like blackbirds that have stolen the seed corn.

Walter loaded the wagon for her that night, and the next morning, after a tearful farewell to Prue, she left for Cedar Springs. The children played in the middle of the wagon and were content for the first half hour; then they began fretting to end their journey. She had little heart to entertain them, but did sing some songs.

She tried to think about what they were going to. There would be good things about it: the place of her own she had wanted so much, maybe some doctor nearby she could work with part of the time, more time to keep a proper house. She'd have time to burn out her skillets, at least.

She wondered what the water would taste like, sweet or bitter, and whether there would be lilac bushes. She could plant a pear tree.

There would be Ral. It would be like starting over, finding out about each other, trying again. She closed her eyes for a minute. *Thank you, Lord, for helping me.*

Then the hot tears came. She thought they would go on forever, rolling down her face until they washed her away. But it was a long way to Cedar Springs, and long before they got there, her eyes were dry.

At least she had her two-dollar stove to keep herself warm.

Epilogue: Fire

Granny always swears by a wood stove for cooking; she says that the food cooked by wood is better. What I remember of her wood cook-stove is her warming oven: curved wrought-iron like a pedestal elevated the two little boxes with their porcelain doors to the level over the rangetop where we have exhaust hoods now. Behind those doors lay treasures: sausages or bacon or ham from breakfast, shelly beans or cornbread from dinner. Nowadays we would fear salmonella or some other bacteria multiplying to epidemic numbers. But I don't remember ever being sick from eating those warm leftovers.

The most prized were biscuits, always delicious. Granny made them in an enamel dishpan that she kept full of flour. I suppose that when she began cooking, she used all-purpose flour: "plain" she called it. But by my time, self-rising flour had become available, and it was her preference; she always tried new products. That didn't mean we agreed on purchases. When she broke her hip at seventy-eight, she was on a mission to return some unbleached flour I had gotten for her. She considered bleached an improvement over the flour of her youth, taken to my grandfather Lanier's mill as wheat and ground as needed. I, on the other hand, in my health-consciousness preferred the less processed.

At any rate, she never gave me a recipe, but she showed me how she made her biscuits. She scooped out a well in the middle of the pan and took hydrogenated shortening (another newfangled replacement, this one for lard), "about a good handful," and worked it patiently into the flour until the right amount was blended. And blending to her was not cutting shortening into flour with a steel pastry blender to make flaky biscuits or pastry: it was using her fingers to warm and rub the flour and shortening together thoroughly, a long, careful process, to assure tender biscuits. Then she put a pinch of soda on top of the mixture and poured on buttermilk, unmeasured but just right. She worked in just the right amount of flour too from the perimeters of the well. She rolled out her biscuits with an amber whiskey bottle that at some time had held a fifth, and she cut them out with a baking-powder can with holes punched in the bottom and baked them on cast-iron bakers, skillets without sides.

The results were always tender and delicious. My sister Jessica preferred her biscuits pale, almost doughy still; I wanted mine brown. Grandad could eat three or four of any color with spicy-hot sausages, then mix a plateful of butter with honey or preserves and spread that on five or six more.

He never gained an ounce of fat, of course; all his life he was all muscle and bone.

I liked the leftovers even better than the biscuits still steaming from the baker. They were crustier after sitting in the drying heat of the warming oven. Grandad and I never agreed about that: he would urge me each morning, "Evelyn, child, eat them up while they're good," and I would always hope that there would be enough left to satisfy my greed in the afternoon, the evening, as my grandparents called everything after two o'clock P.M.

So we made our choices.

And ultimately I choose to make my own kind of biscuits, flaky from the unhandled, refrigerated shortening—margarine, not the white hydrogenated stuff. Even my self-rising flour is unbleached and, heresy of heresies, mixed with oat bran. I do use buttermilk, so perhaps I am not totally depraved. And the one heirloom I begged from my grandmother was her whiskey-bottle rolling pin. But I express my will.

The wood fire that cooked Granny's food also warmed her kitchen, and when it was replaced first with oil and then with fireless electricity, she turned to other fuels for heating the house. But when the frost of old age chilled her bones, she again had a wood stove put in her living room. She said that nothing else warmed her as it did. And there was a pleasure in that baking heat, even in the extremes to which she took it, making December like July.

Her wood fire also almost burned her house down once. The carpet bears the black marks where a log she was putting into the stove slipped away from her and charred into the wooden floor underneath before she wrestled it back into the stove with the tongs and her withered strength. Fire is a dangerous servant.

Prometheus, the Greeks' mythic fire-bringer, expresses the many uses and the great destructiveness of fire. He was judged a benefactor by men, but by the gods a criminal deserving of eternal, excruciating pain. Lucifer, the Hebrew bearer of light, presents a similar ambiguity. And this is inherent in the nature of fire. It warms, nurtures, illuminates, refines, purifies, and protects; but it also injures and destroys.

The passion that warms our hearts consumes us.

In our lives we learn to handle the danger. "The burnt child dreads the fire." Do we ever learn to handle that internal fire, the will that tempts us to choose the fruit that makes us as gods, the fruit that makes us mortal?

Acknowledgments

Again, I want to thank my family, my colleagues, and other friends who have encouraged and contributed in various ways to my writing. Members of my writers' group heard the bulk of this story early; Don Goss, Jim Hiett, Jeanne Irelan, Dan Jewell, and Al Lawler were then the principal members. I also value very highly the help and encouragement of Reynolds Price.

In addition to my grandmother Proctor, who gave me stories, information, and language for all my early books, my mother has shared reminiscences. I also am grateful to Don Goss, Betty Langston Hawkins, Evelyn Kincade Hiett, James G. Hiett, Sr., Joyce Jewell, Marie Proctor, and Debra Whitaker for family stories or information.

At Volunteer State Community College, Larry Gay Reagan, Jim Hiett, and Dan Jewell have been liberal with help and encouragement in production of the manuscript, and the library staff has been helpful and forgiving.

241

As always, my editor Sandra McCormack has contributed wisely to the book. Calvert Morgan has been patient and helpful. Sabrina Soares has been a careful copyeditor, as she was on *Private Knowledge*.

I continue to be grateful to the teachers who encouraged me and contributed to my development. From high school I remember particularly Marie Moore, Florence Hunnicutt, Carlee Kerley Deasy, Lawrence Bradley, Robbie Woodall, Reba Jernigan, Robert Dawson, Augusta Empson, Maxine Jenkins Shannon, and Frances and William Hunter.

The title for each book comes from the writings of a Victorian poet. "The Heart Asks Pleasure First" is from Emily Dickinson, Number 536; "What a Dusty Answer" is from George Meredith, *Modern Love*, 50; "The Birthday of My Life" is from Christina Rossetti's "A Birthday"; and "The Pain of Finite Hearts" is from Robert Browning's "Two in the Campagna."

Books that I can recognize as contributing to the background of the novel are *Only Yesterday* by Frederick Lewis Allen; *American Chronicle* by Lois and Alan Gordon; and *DuPont: One Hundred and Forty Years* by William S. Dutton.

Formerly published in *Number One* were excerpts called "Horses," "Fooling Around," and the first three pages of "The Heart Asks Pleasure First"; I thank the editors for permission to reprint them.